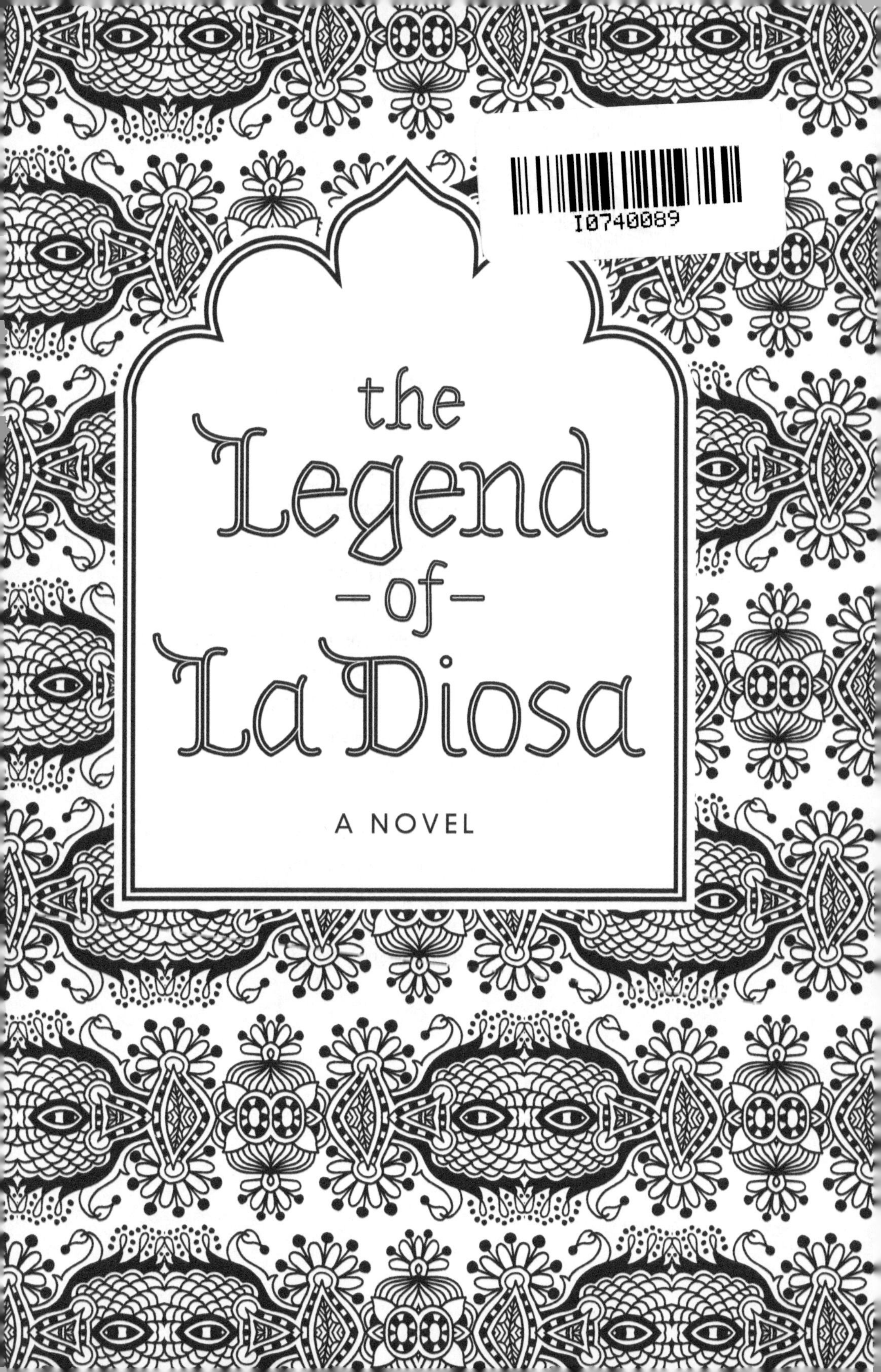

the
Legend
-of-
La Diosa
A NOVEL

ALSO BY CHUCK ROSENTHAL

THE SHORTEST FAREWELLS ARE THE BEST (FLASH NOIR WITH GAIL WRONSKY, 2015)

TEN THOUSAND HEAVENS (2013)

TOMORROW YOU'LL BE ONE OF US (SCI-FI POEMS WITH GAIL WRONSKY, 2013)

WEST OF EDEN: A LIFE IN 21ST CENTURY LOS ANGELES (2012)

COYOTE O'DONOHUGHE'S HISTORY OF TEXAS (2010)

ARE WE NOT THERE YET?: TRAVELS IN NEPAL, NORTH INDIA, AND BHUTAN (2009)

THE HEART OF MARS (2008)

THE LOOP TRILOGY (AUTHOR'S ORIGINAL EDITION, 2007):

LOOP'S PROGRESS—EXPERIMENTS WITH LIFE AND DEAF—LOOP'S END

NEVER LET ME GO: A MEMOIR (2004)

MY MISTRESS, HUMANITY (2002)

JACK KEROUAC'S AVATAR ANGEL: HIS LAST NOVEL (2001)

ELENA OF THE STARS (1995)

LOOPS END (1992)

EXPERIMENTS WITH LIFE AND DEAF (1987)

LOOPS PROGRESS (1986)

the Legend of La Diosa

A NOVEL

CHUCK ROSENTHAL

LettersAt3amPress

The Legend of La Diosa
Copyright © 2016 by Chuck Rosenthal
Publisher's Preface Copyright © 2016 by Michael Ventura

Portions of *The Legend of La Diosa* have appeared in the *Catamaran
Literary Reader*, *Chicago Quarterly Review*, and *Intellectual Refuge*. The
author gratefully acknowledges the support of editors Elizabeth McKenzie,
Catherine Segurson, and Christopher Schnieders, as well as my publishers,
Jazmin Aminian and Michael Ventura. Appreciation to my designer,
Ash Goodwin. Thanks to Beyond Baroque Literary Arts Venue and the
Catamaran Writers Conference where much of this work had its debut.

All rights reserved. No reproduction of this work can be made
without permission of the Author or Publisher. This is a work
of fiction. Names, characters, places and incidents are either
the products of the author's imagination or are used fictitiously.
Any resemblance to anyone living or dead is coincidental.

Paperback ISBN: 978-0-9914648-8-3
Ebook ISBN: 978-0-9914648-9-0

Library of Congress Control Number: 2016937794

Published in 2016 by LettersAt3amPress
Box 93
Meadow Vista, CA 95722
editor@3amproductions.org

Publisher/Editors: Jazmin Aminian Jordán, Michael Ventura
Editor-At-Large: Rebekah J. Morton
Social Media Manager: Ashley C. Aminian
Book and Jacket Designer: Ash Goodwin, www.ashgood.com
Cover Art: *Sri Radha alone* by Srimati Syamarani Dasi. Copyright
Syamarani dasi, painted under the guidance of Srila Bhaktivedanta
Narayana Gosvami Maharaja, www.bhaktiart.net, used with permission.

All poems attributed to La Diosa were written by
Gail Wronsky; the others are by Chuck Rosenthal;
lines in italics were taken from Gail Wronsky's work.

FOR GAIL, ALWAYS AND INEVITABLY

PUBLISHER'S PREFACE

Chuck Rosenthal's *The Legend of La Diosa* is a fast drive around a tight curve powered by the *momentum* of love—how love sways you, jolts you, and makes you thoroughly unfit for the quotidian. You feel like you've known this brand new person forever because you have.

Kind of crazy but not at all flighty, because love is life or death and Chuck Rosenthal knows this. He also knows love is playful (or we couldn't bear it), so this story invites us to play in a realm where what's happened to us "might not matter at all and yet meant everything whether it mattered or not."

In Rosenthal's writing there's always music just on the other side of the page. His language cavorts as *The Legend of La Diosa* spins its audacious tall tale to focus on happiness as a *value*. Not many writers dare this because happiness is damned hard to write (and because writers famously know little about it).

It all happens "there, on the firing line between nothingness and the divine"—and isn't that just like love?

—Michael Ventura

the Legend -of- La Diosa

THE LEGEND OF LA DIOSA: BEGINS

BEFORE THE POET, La Diosa, became Roscoe Harlan's lover, she danced upon the bones of a hundred men. In the beginning Diosa was known simply as Lisa Hornstein, Lisa Hornstein from Harrisburg, Pennsylvania, whose father, Henry, worked in middle management for GM and whose mother, JoAnne, who changed her name to Joan (of Arc), believed that both her sons, one older than Lisa and one younger, that both of them were the Second Coming of Jesus; neither of them turned out to be Jesus, as you probably figured, but Joan, decades before it became chic in Malibu and elsewhere, stopped singing Christmas Carols while she vacuumed, songs in which she'd substituted the names of her sons, first Norman, then Archie, for Jesus, and began channeling messages from the saints, who happened to work vaguely in iambic

1

pentameter, some might call it doggerel, an odd form for the saints to work in, but many of the saints were not well educated (or as the Angel Gabriel said to Mohammed, "I'm speaking to you in Arabic so you'll understand") and Joan made Lisa copy down her inspirations word for word after school—there are volumes of it somewhere—though oddly, Joan also read Shakespeare and Robert Louis Stevenson to Lisa, as well as Dr. Seuss. Years passed. Until one day, a pre-teen teen Lisa, on the verge of insanity herself, refused to copy anymore and Joan decided that the only way around the problem was for her and the three kids to commit group suicide. Lisa could tell, because her mother sang, "We thought your first son was Christ savior, but he just didn't have the behavior. You thought your next son was Christ Lord, but saving the world made him bored. Your daughter won't write your cosmic insight. They don't believe you're Joan of Arc, they think that you're insane. So now there's nothing left to do but park them in front of a train."

"Want to go for a car-bye?" Joan asked them all after school the next day. "Want some ice cream pie?"

"Yeah!" said Norman.

"Sure!" said Archie.

"Uh-uh," said Lisa.

"You scream, I scream. We all scream for ice cream!" said Joan.

"Right after I go to the bathroom," said Lisa, and she crawled out the bathroom window. Years later, after several failed suicide attempts of her own, Diosa regretted not having let her mother take the whole suicide thing out of her hands, but back then she was just a kid. So when her father got home she pulled him aside and told him *everything.* Everything. He put Lisa in a mental institution.

Wrong-headed as it seemed to Lisa at the time, putting her in a mental institution helped Joan get a little better. Call it transference even if it ain't.

Lisa met some interesting people in the mental institution, many of whom, all men, believed they were Jesus. Most of them, much like Flannery O'Connor's Misfit, seemed to have exploited the fine line between saving people's souls and murdering them. Women were much more interested in suicide, something that prompted Lisa to an early sociological insight: men murder, women commit suicide. She used to sit and play cards with one murderer named Jimmy Joe who looked a little like a squat Elvis Presley. He believed he was Jesus and that all the hits on the radio were stolen from him.

"Know that song, 'Feelings'?" said Jimmy Joe.

"Yes, I do," said Lisa Hornstein.

"I wrote that."

"It's a lousy song," Lisa said.

"Doesn't change anything about its origin," Jimmy Joe said.

"I suppose it doesn't," Lisa said.

"Ever heard of a guy named Jesus?" said Jimmy Joe. "That's me."

Jimmy Joe Jesus shared smuggled cigarettes with her, then he shared some beer, then he tried to fuck her and then he tried to strangle her. That's the short of it. Her other friend, a girl a little older than her named Rosie, had carved all the names of her ex-boyfriends onto her thighs with a razor blade. It took Lisa a little while to figure out that the boyfriends were made up. Rosie slit her wrists and got transferred to a more serious situation. Well, as we all know, insanity wasn't invented by insane asylums, it was just codified by them. Anyway, a little about insanity goes a long way.

Lisa got out of insane school knowing the code. Her parents moved to Detroit where she went to Groves High and joined the cheerleaders. At half-time of their first football game against Birmingham, she went up to the second floor bathroom where she knew she could smoke a Marlboro and be alone. She ran into the captain of the Birmingham cheerleaders, Madonna. Madonna had dark hair and dark eyeliner. She held a joint to her lips and a bottle of sloe gin at her knee. "Here," she said with the joint.

They got stoned as shit and drank sloe gin in the bathroom. They blew pot smoke out the window into the ghostly parking lot night where Madonna pointed beyond the bleachers to the parked cars and said, "See those girls out there hanging on boys?"

"Sober as asphalt," said Lisa. "Stupid and joyous."

"I like your way with words," Madonna said. "They're heading for nothing but no good. Disasters waiting to happen." She reached under her cheerleading sweater and pulled out several delicate chains from which hung gold crosses. "Cheerleaders and crosses are a good mix," Madonna said.

"Can I have one of those?" Lisa said.

"You sure can." And Madonna gave Lisa a chain and cross. She put it around Lisa's neck. "It's you," she said. She guzzled the end of the sweet, red gin, as red as her lipstick. "I like big cars," Madonna said. "I like the back seats of big cars."

"Bang, slam, thank you man," Lisa said.

Madonna raised her pom-poms. "Bam, bam, go Birmingham!" she said.

That night during the game the school photographer took pictures. Lisa's mom kept that picture of her forever. She put it on her dresser next to her own wedding picture; Lisa grinning, her wavy brown hair falling around her cheeks, pom-poms raised in front of her, a gold cross dangling at her neck against her green cheerleading sweater, eyes like slits, stoned as shit.

(That night a boy in the stands went home and just like Rosie carved the words *Lisa* and *Diosa* on the inside of his thigh. He showed it to Lisa).

"Who's that?"

"That's you," he said.

In the next four years over a hundred boys at Groves High would wear the scars *Lisa* and *Diosa* somewhere on their body. (And it was years before she even thought of changing her name).

Madonna became Madonna. Lisa Hornstein became a poet. If entertainers never find out who they are because they're too busy being somebody, then poets die on the cross of the self. Got a cross in your room? If Jesus is on there, you're Catholic. If nobody's on there, you're Protestant. If you're on there, you're a poet. It doesn't matter if you're any good (though it might). It's a soul thing. That was the difference between Madonna and Diosa who did not become fast friends, who, in fact, never met again.

That crucifix of the self was something that attracted Diosa to male poets, that willingness to kill themselves instead of somebody else. Call it their feminine side. And their deep, deep, deep need of romance, a constant need to fall in love and fall in love again, to become victims of inspiration and re-inspiration. The difference between a poet and a Casanova was the same as the difference between a poet and an entertainer.

The poet killed himself with love. Killed himself for love. And you had to love that. You had to love them loving you, doing that to themselves as they loved you, even if it meant they were not good lovers, nor faithful lovers, for they were enthralled by romance, by the self-indulgence of romance, the self-indulgence of slow suicide. Even when she came to understand that placing oneself on a crucifix was an act of self-worship, that to murder oneself is to immortalize one's self, it didn't change the heat.

And for their part, poets, among others, loved Diosa, too, as she grew into an alluring young woman, enchanting, quick-witted, multi-furtive.

Other than this chance meeting with Diosa, you probably know more about Madonna than I do, and almost as much, or more, as she knows about herself, except for the fact that when they met, Madonna was a year older than Diosa and now she's several years younger. Actually, you probably aren't aware of the film made of Madonna in high school in which an egg was fried on her stomach, though by now I suppose it's probably on You Tube.

In high school, Lisa Hornstein was so beautiful as to be feared by boys. It happens a lot. A lot of men are afraid of women. A lot of men hate them. If most men reach sexual maturity by fifteen, then it is at fifteen when they settle into the anxieties of their sexual irresolution, when their attraction to other men is twisted into homophobia, and in reaction, their attraction to women settles into possessiveness, fear, aggression. Women never learn this. If they did, it would end the species. Like a lot of truly beautiful girls, Lisa felt isolated and unattractive. Nice boys feared her and bored her. The bad boys she was attracted to scared her. They stole cars and carried guns. Though she thought it might be nice to steal some cars and carry a gun.

The summer between high school and college Lisa took a summer job in Mackinac City at the tip of Michigan. She did it to get away from her mother; normal enough, though in Lisa's case a run for cover.

The shop was owned by an older woman, a widow, Mrs. Kisilinski. It was filled with tourist stuff: replicas of the Mackinaw Island Bridge, snow bubbles of Michigan with a star for Mackinaw City, paintings of the Last Supper surrounded by cheap sea shells from Florida. Mostly, she sold fudge. She stayed in a boarding house where she had a room and shared a bath with two gymnasts from Bowling Green, Ohio. They were easy to ignore. She spent her time after work walking along the shore or standing in the park near the great bridge and gazing over the huge, blue expanse of lake and sky stretching out to Lake Huron and Lake Michigan. She began to write some things down. *The eyes of men,* she wrote, *are verdant with disgrace.* Her words were so like whispers, it was as if she could barely hear them, barely tell what they meant. Yet a virgin, already she was dreaming of infidelity.

It was an uneventful month but for a dark-skinned young man who visited the store, though that was uneventful, too, at least at first. He was slender, often unkempt, but sometimes not. He always wore long, dark blue chinos and Birkenstocks with white socks, a button-down shirt covered by a sweater, even in the summer heat. He came almost every day. Occasionally he bought goat milk fudge. Sometimes he bought nothing at all. He watched her over the shelves of bric-a-brac, under dark brow, and she found his eyes full of pleading; if not gentle, then at least pleading, for she began to notice him slipping things into the pockets of his pants.

She felt sorry for him and let him steal. She imagined him stealing to help support his mother, or a family. He'd turn as he left the store and catch her eye and she felt that if there was not much good she could do in the world, then she could permit this, this indiscretion which would right an imbalance. Until the old woman took inventory and accused her of stealing, or at least permitting it.

Oh, you know where this goes, don't you? Roscoe has told himself in the past that a good story, a well-told one, is so webbed full of causality that you don't notice it. That's why, I've answered on too many occasions, the good ones go untold, or if told, unread, if read, misunderstood. Give me simplicity or give me death!

Lisa took the hit for the young man. She said she didn't know who was stealing from the shelves. She got fired. She helped Mrs. Kisilinski close the store, then Mrs. Kisilinski subtracted the stolen inventory from her pay. She owed Mrs. Kisilinski eight dollars. "We'll call it even," Mrs. Kisilinski said without looking up from the register. Lisa took off her badge that said *Lisa* and put it on the counter. She didn't want to be Lisa Hornstein anymore.

When she left the store that night, he was waiting for her. It was not quite dusk. Mrs. Kisilinski watched from the window as the young man took Lisa's hand.

"Thank you," the young man said. "But it was unnecessary."

Lisa withdrew her hand. She said, "Would you like to walk to the bridge?"

She turned and walked. He followed her at first, then came up next to her, keeping his pace a shoulder ahead as if trying to lead a horse, had she known then about leading horses, though she did not. But she did not like him surging ahead of her and she stopped. When he noticed, he turned, offered a partial grin. At the bridge the fading sun was behind them in the southwest. It made the water silver and cast the arching shadow of the bridge onto the lakes. A wind rustled the August leaves, already turned down and drying in nascent autumn. She stepped in front of him to the railing and stared out to the water and sky.

"You didn't need it," she said.

"No." He stepped up next to her again. "It is not proper for a girl to stand up for a man."

She stood on the edge of space, in the vice of opposites called the desire of men. In the dozens of times she'd watched him steal and met his gaze, she'd fallen deeper into the debt he owed her. No woman, not even Diosa, understood a man's desire, but she felt a chilling grip at her spine now, as if someone had pinned her wings in a fist.

"If I wept for you," she said to him, "would these lakes long for my tears?"

"My deeds are mine and your deeds are yours," he said.

She understood now that she shouldn't have walked to work. She should have driven or rode her bike. She should have left the store the moment she was fired, in the daylight, instead of waiting for Mrs. Kisilinski to compute her pay and helping to close the store. She should not have let him touch her, not have invited him for the walk, though she now understood he would have followed her anyway. Now it was dark. Now there was no one around and the city park stretched between her and the boarding house.

"Would you steal dark from darkness?" Lisa Hornstein said. "Light from light? Steal breath?" How could he know it was a curse when she did not? She turned away from him. He grabbed her shoulder and spun her to face him. She stepped back. He grabbed her by the neck, put an arm around her throat and a hand over her mouth. He dragged her into the park and raped her. And when he was done, he pinned her head to the ground by her hair and dripped his sperm on her lips. "God created the sexes," he said, "the male and the female, from a drop of ejected semen."

The young man, named Mohamed McGhee, went home to his

young wife, Sharid, who that very day, after months of complaining of mysterious illnesses which often kept her from having sex, had gotten him to take her to the Division of Motor Vehicles to apply for a driver's permit, a necessity she argued, for an American wife who would shop for the family, with children who need to go to the doctor and need to go to school, all while he was at work. The Holy Book simply hadn't anticipated this car thing. You had to make a lot of inferences to keep women from behind the wheel. It was a lot easier in Saudi Arabia or Utah where you had a whole society benevolently protecting them. He conceded. She waited behind him at the DMV, her tan face peering timidly out, but her brown eyes sparkling behind her wire rim glasses. He spoke first. He answered all the questions unless she had to answer them. He wrote the check. Yet when they called her for her photograph, she stepped in front of him and walked to the camera. She stood on the yellow line and beamed.

At first, after the rape, Mohamed's lust for the teenager from the fudge store seemed sated, then it aroused a passion in him for Sharid. He took her that night, as well. Then he despised her. He hated his work at IBM where he designed software. He dreamed of moving his family to southern Utah and keeping several wives who did not drive cars. He thought of the girl. In the middle of the night he left his apartment and went back to the place where he'd taken her. He knelt on the impression of her body in the grass, smelling the ground. She had given herself to him. Even if she didn't know. She'd been brought to him by He who knew all, controlled all. Not a baby was born who was not in His thoughts. Not a moment passed anywhere in the universe that was not the beat of His heart.

Yet how each of us walked in our own doom. Cities and nations had been brought down because they had turned from God. She had put out her hand. Touched him. Followed him. Led him. Day after day her eyes touched his eyes. How could he have known she was a dark angel, a whore, that he had been in her spell? "I am not responsible for your actions," said the Book, "and you are not responsible for mine." God had made the world perfectly good. Placed the sun to light the day and the moon the night, blanketed the black sky with bejeweled stars, spread animals and plants over the earth to feed and clothe His people. Only the will of men brought evil into this bounty.

Mohamed McGhee walked to the bridge. If he could have the girl again, he would. If he could kill her now, he would. But instead he carried her in his heart like a hive of bees; until his death she would make honey of his sin. God brings whom He will into His mercy. He whom God leads astray has no one to protect him. It is a long way down from the top of the bridge to the water, which is flat and hard like cement. He plans to think of God as he flies, but he does not. He sees the girl before his flying eyes, and a hundred bleeding boys, a name carved on their thighs. He spreads his arms and ever so briefly thinks he is an angel flying headlong in front of a great army of believers; maybe he is, but as the water comes close he is overcome by the anguish of a man desperately, hopelessly in love.

This is not a story. This is truth; a few inspired lines brought forth by metaphor, by parable, by prayer, by trick, by fever, by example; this was a sample; Mohamed McGhee, just a couple of words on a page. A man who raped a girl in Mackinac City, Michigan, and committed suicide by jumping off the Mackinac Island Bridge. Two lives were conceived that night, as well. One was Ramsey McGhee, the son of Sharid, who put her grief in God's hands, got her driver's license, and drove to Ann Arbor where she started school and went to work in a bagel shop. She became a civil rights lawyer. Ramsey, after some obstinate teenage years, re-converted to Islam and became a famous intellectual and apologist for his faith.

Lisa Hornstein found the police worse than the rape. She was ridiculed and probed, and cut off by her interrogator before she could finish her sentences. The interrogating officer was female. Lisa quickly surmised that the fact that she'd walked off alone with a thief made her more culpable than him. If knowledge is a community affair, then McGhee was right, it wasn't his fault. She didn't find out she was pregnant until she reached college almost a month later, in Kalamazoo. Her first sex. Her first abortion.

In college at Kalamazoo, Diosa, still Lisa Hornstien then, took a boyfriend, a sweet kid named Ralph Hopper who she called Hoppie, a high school All-American soccer player, not that it meant much back then. After he met Lisa he quit the soccer team and joined the Kalamazoo College All-Kazoo Marching Band, an act of such self-conscious irrelevancy that it bored her. Things fell apart. Hoppie dropped out of school and joined the navy; Diosa always thought of him as her first and dearest love, her Michael Furey; in the navy he became a brilliant F-15 pilot, but without a war to fight evolved into a flight instructor, then a member of the Blue Angels; one day, his heart aching, his jet a singing cross in the burning sky, he broke formation and took his final dive. (Not so many years later, on the Night of Ghosts, Roscoe sat on Diosa's bed in her apartment in Salt Lake City, across from the cemetery, and watched out the crack of her bedroom door as she sat in candle light with her Amontillado, watched as her dead lovers came to her door with their gifts: a pedant of amethyst, a camel's saddlebag, a spider's silken dream, the last thought of a dying child—what can you do with gifts from the dead? you turn them into poems, into eternity—Hoppie, her first love, was the last to come, his arms full of red gladiolas stolen from a grave).

She tried lesbianism. Her lover, a jovial, pretty girl who called herself Pheda Lamort, was an apprentice of Conrad Hilberry. Together Pheda and Lisa got high and read Walt Whitman, Emily Dickinson, Gertrude Stein, Virginia Woolf, Leonora Carrington, Sylvia Plath, Adrienne Rich. Lisa changed her name to Lisa Diosa. She stopped shaving. Got a crew cut. Bought all her clothes from thrift stores and wore army boots. The two of them tromped through Kalamazoo, boots trucking, long, black coats flapping, yelling "Fuck you!" It attracted boys like flies. (Years later Roscoe's closest boyhood friend, when visiting him in Los Angeles, upon spotting a picture of Pheda Lamort on Diosa's bookshelf, fell hopelessly in love, sold his business, left his wife and children and moved to Kalamazoo where Pheda kept residence; he threw everything he had into a small press dedicated to publishing lesbian poetry. The press went belly up almost immediately. Pheda Lamort gained weight and disappeared inside her self, and Roscoe's boyhood friend moved to Seattle and became a coffee mogul). For her part, during her sophomore year, Diosa brought Pheda home for Thanksgiving. She announced that she'd changed her last name from Hornstein to Diosa. Her parents pulled her out of Kalamazoo and sent her to the University of Virginia in Charlottesville.

Where she took up anthropology. Her professor, Simone Peter Dubois, fell in love with her, though he was twice her age. He had a job. He bought her presents. He dreamed of Africa. Diosa dreamed she was a cat. At night, she walked along the fence outside his window, silver and silken, preening her long fur, her call to him like something carnal in his ears, *what color is the blue weeping of hyacinths?* He ran his hands through his thick, blond hair, held his face, left his wife. Traveled to Africa and learned to speak in short, guttural clicks. Upon his return, he was to take Diosa with him on his next trip to the Kalahari (but while he was gone, a young Chilean, Arturo Cruz, who claimed to be the National Chilean Surf Champion, met her at a bar and she went home with him; she made him so insane with love that he crawled across the walls and ceiling of his bedroom like a spider; he crawled over her; he sunk his mandibles into her neck; it was the first time she came; he took her to the coast and upon his surf board stood with her upon his shoulders atop a seething wave; from there, turning her head from the shore, she saw the shores of France, the shadow of Paris like an insect on the edge of a web; by the time they reached the sand she couldn't love him anymore, couldn't drink anymore Brazilian liquorices; at night, he felt like something tiny that she would eventually have to eat; and so he stalked her; he slept at her door, his breath sucking through the keyhole, his fingers slipping through the crack on the floor, until he followed her one night to the bar where they'd met and the owner, Sandobar Ohara, an erudite book lover and restaurateur, saw the look of fear and tedium in Diosa's eyes when she entered his establishment, Arturo Cruz panting at her side like something once ferocious and now a whelp; Sandobar lifted his finger and had Cruz knocked out and put on an airplane leaving D.C. with a liberal senator bound for Colima, Mexico; everyone on the small jet died when the pilot, thinking he'd spotted the tiny airfield in the fog, crashed into a forest strung with lights). Simone Peter Dubois returned from Africa and Diosa saw that he was different in that way that men who have not changed believe they have changed.

"I am a shaman," he said.

"What did you have to do?"

"Stay awake for three days and nights, then eat the raw rectum of a skunk." She later found out there were no skunks in Africa and he must have eaten the rectum of an African polecat. It only made things worse.

Diosa put her index finger on his lips. She held him there at arms length. She turned away and left the Department of Anthropology. Simone Peter Dubois disappeared in the Kalahari.

Enter Sandobar Ohara who feted her with pheasant, *Chateaubriand* and French wine, taught her to drink chilled martinis straight up with only a breath of dry vermouth and a lemon twist. She grew her hair long again, read all of Shakespeare and Colette. A short, dapper man, Ohara wanted her totally, completely; he was that kind of man; he wanted her so much he bought the thrift stores where she bought her clothes, the bookstores where she bought her books. *All men are in love with me, she wrote, their eyes like caves, their skeletal fingers savage on my pelvis bone.* He wanted her all over him; her thick hair a hairfall around him, he came before she could unzip his pants, she on top, or else he could only come on her stomach when she wore hose and heels, which was fine with her but for the hose and heels. "Oh Sandy," she said to him, "I have too much hair." He took her to New York where she ran off with a Jamaican boy, barely seventeen, a model who had slept with Liza Minelli, Michael Jackson, Mick Jagger; he wore eyeliner and lip gloss, platform shoes with heels of glass. His loving was frail and quick, but maybe that was better. She came to find the fickle wand of manhood far too fickle. By the time she returned to Sandy's hotel in Chelsea, the boy had slit his wrists with the broken shards of his heels and Sandy lay naked upon his bed, weeping, his diminutive stick hard in the air. She mounted him. He came. Back in Charlottesville, she stopped seeing him for a while. "You're not leaving me," he said. And sensing something now, both inside her and outside her, she whispered, "No, I am never leaving anyone. Ever am I leaving no one. Never am I leaving ever leaving." She went back to her Richmond apartment and wrapped herself in scarves and lay in bed. She sat at her window watching the cars on the gray street. In a month she discovered she was pregnant and put on her long black coat at dawn and walked through an uncommon blizzard to Sandy's door. "You're back," he said. And she said, "I'm pregnant." He told her to wait there. She heard the laughter of a girl. He brought her two hundred fifty dollars. He said, "That should be enough." But a funeral costs more than that. The fetus had been male and that night Sandobar Ohara lay in his bed like a fish, suffocating on air.

She dyed her hair brown and red. Her hair poured from her like a jungle. She moved to a cottage in the country, across from a field of cows. She opened the wire fence and let them rove onto her land. They came to her porch, then came onto her porch. She brought them inside and let them watch her cook, carrot and lentil soup, brown bread, rice. They folded up and slept on her living room floor, murring gently to her when she petted their soft rubber noses. On warm afternoons she walked with them in the fields and they followed her in a line with their rolling behemothical bodies on their spindly legs walk, speaking to her of fur and grass and milk. Then, as if they had all been impregnated by a ghost, at night she heard them praying for their unborn children. "What are you afraid of?" she asked them. Loss, they murred. Loss. But she really didn't know anything about cows. She didn't know any more about cows than the cows had taught her. The babies came. She watched them struggle to their feet, follow their mothers. They bounced against each other, bounded, their round brown eyes and fur like satin. Her landlord, Mathieu Valbuena, a famous and now wealthy poet at UVA, who as a boy accidentally shot his brother in the woods, an act from which he never recovered and wrote about over and over and over in poems which had gradually shrunk in size over the years from pages long to a few mere lines from which, if you knew his work at all, you could understand the allusions to the rest of his opus, an eventuality which caused him tremendous guilt of which he wrote about with even greater success. Valbuena came for the rent.

"I can't pay it," she said. "I don't have a job."

"I thought you were a student," he said.

"Of cows," she said.

"Don't you know what they do with these cows?" he said to her.

But at that moment her blue eyes opened an eternity to him and he knew that he could teach her everything about poems and she could teach him everything about cows. Of course, he was wrong about both, but it was deeply felt and it made him walk away without the rent and with the memory of her eyes, her face turned toward him slightly with the wisdom of a doe. When he went home to his wife, a painter, and his two young daughters, his life as he'd known it had already come to an end.

"Rent?" said his wife, Margarite.

"I might as well be dead," he said to her.

"You've only fallen in love again," she said, because she'd come to learn that he fell in love again and again, that he shot his brother again and again, and if he did not kill and did not fall in love, if he were not burdened with heart aching guilt, then he would not write and there'd be no salary from UVA, and if divorce were a possibility, well, not yet,

not while their daughters were so young, besides, she had as much or
more to lose as he, this house, a mansion in the country, given to them
by her parents, now half in his name, and as well the land where the girl
rented the cottage; before this she'd learned enough and took a lover in
New York City where two galleries showed her work, but her trips to
the city, once a month, were financed by the rent. But unlike his wife,
Valbuena couldn't simply take a lover, have an affair, go to the Y and
have a steam bath before coming home.

He ran his hands through his thick, black hair. He sat, elbows on his
knees, his hands covering his face, fingertips pressed against his eyes. He
raised his head. The world was new.

"This isn't like the others," he said.

"They never are," said Margarite. "You have to pick up your
daughters from school."

He arose. The simple duties of his life now like walking on sand, no,
a desert of sand through which he walked, his back laden with his own
gravestone.

"Are you going to cry?" she said.

"I'll get them," he sniffled. If his greatness could be measured by
how well he carried the desperate misfortune and horrible pain he
often brought upon himself, then he was a great man, and a good one,
too. But this time, this time, after all those times his love had been
overwrought and his reaction overblown, this time he was right.

When he left for the girls, Margarite got up from her five-by-five
canvas of huge brown and gold flowers which tumbled over each other
in such profusion that the decorative became abstract and the abstract
disconcerting, and the disconcern, if you kept looking, troublesome, she
got up and went to her Volvo station wagon and drove out to the cottage

where she saw the girl standing in the pasture among the mothers and their calves, the spring sun splaying the air as if it were raining knives, the cows murmuring in that aching, prescient way, and the girl lopping away chunks of her own hair with a pair of huge scissors. Margarite, hating her already, hated her in a way she hadn't hated the others. The others were only girl poets. This was a young goddess.

Margarite crossed the field, the high grass scratching at her naked calves left exposed by her Capri pants. She walked up to Diosa, who stood in the pile of her own hair.

Margarite said to her, "These calves become veal."

"Do you think I'm cutting my hair for my own good?" Diosa said.

"They are separated from their mothers, isolated, over-stuffed, then slaughtered."

"Do you think it's a metaphor for young women?" Diosa asked. "Do cows choose to be cows? Veal meat?"

"Sleeping with Mathieu will not make you a famous poet," Margarite said.

"Who is a poet?" Diosa said.

And Diosa, who already suspected this was some wife, in fact, Valbuena's wife, because only men with wives lost their hearts so completely, Valbuena had—death leaping from a past self like a cat on fire, his heart dropping in front of her, his pleading hands speaking to the air, his brow whispering—Diosa said, "Will it keep me from becoming a famous poet the way the world keeps a refrigerator from becoming an elephant?" She lopped off a chunk of brown hair and blew it from her hand, because what do you tell a wife who has confronted you with her husband's love? That you want him? That you do not want him? Which is the greater insult? "Would you prefer a hollow man or a dead man?" she finally said to Margarite. "What have I done," she asked, "but stand here and cut my hair among cows?"

They came that night and took the calves. She heard the rumbling of the trucks and the baleful moaning of the mothers, the bleating of the calves, while some unknown part of her ran from herself, and instead of leaping from her porch to throw her body between the men and the babies, she slept on, awaking in the morning with blood on her swollen tongue. The mothers swayed and moaned for two weeks until slowly, like the groan of a departing train, it lay on the edge of her hearing. She couldn't walk among them anymore. She gave up vegetarianism. She jumped into her rattling Volkswagen Rabbit and drove to fraternity row, parked, and walked into a party. There, she spotted a thin young man with long, wavy hair, wearing a sleeveless t-shirt and a bow tie. His eyes were gentle and witty, his pants linen, his shoes Italian, and he had his arm around another young man with short curly hair, the two of them swaying a bit drunkenly to Roxy Music and the soft voice of Brian Ferry. She liked Roxy Music and she liked Brian Ferry. The young man's name was Jonathan Chrisman Swift, yes, one of the meatpacking Swifts. She walked up to him. "Marry me," she said. And he did.

Soon afterward, at the English Department at UVA, she found Mathieu Valbuena in his office and stood in front of his desk with her many lengths of hair and mascara flying across her face like black rain. "Let me study poetry," she said.

Mathieu Valbuena's heart leapt like a hunter's behind a deer blind, his finger soft upon the trigger, his blood like mercury, his lungs liquid lead; exhale, then squeeze, don't tug.

He looked Diosa in the eye. "You were an anthropology major," he said. "What have you read? What have you written?"

Diosa picked up a pencil from Valbuena's desk, and a blank sheet of paper. She stooped over and wrote:

The Immense Jolt of Loving

For you the simulations of my mental instability become untranslatable. For you in the face of the air that separates us I purchase a revolver. I spit, I shut, I kick the curtains, the bolts, the forest of doors. You are sexual copper. You lie like a rose on our bed of poetic manifestations. Do you find me charming or idiotic? All this lavishness. Too much biting in the middle of the night? I've put the photographic plate of my face into an acid bath. You'll be shocked by what emerges, more or less. The bones of one continuous escape.

She handed it to Mathieu Valbuena who shook as he read, his eyes filling with something more profound than admiration, deeper than jealousy, more avaricious than love. Almost unconsciously he held out his trembling hand. "Maybe we can talk about this," he said. He choked. "Over lunch." Lunch. The door to love.

And Diosa put out her hand, too, touching the tip of his middle finger with a purple nail, her wedding ring shining like a poet's moon. She began to hum something, an old show tune, something from musical theater, she could barely remember. "How does that go?" she whispered. "A boy like you . . ." But that was all. And that's how Diosa came to study poetry and, in her way, saved Valbuena's life.

Yet after that moment Mathieu Valbuena became as an abandoned shell. When he tried to speak, his voice became a choking gasp. His thoughts, now like effigies of mannequins, fell invisibly upon the page. He drove himself mad with love poems that died on his fingertips, metaphors that became drool on his lips, similes that collapsed inside themselves before he could raise a comparison. His wife left him. Both of his children went mad. His life thus saved, he became a body builder. A marathon runner. A tri-athlete. He tried to sing opera. Learned Greek. But he did not write again for twenty years. Swift, it turned out, was gay, but not gay enough to save his own life. There is more to come. Much more. But for Lisa Diosa it was yet the unknowable beginning of something. Her slouching toward Roscoe Harlan.

ROSCOE EMERGE

THERE WAS SOMETHING ghostly about the sound of trains, so it seemed to him, though maybe it was less the sound, the moaning in the night, whistling through the black streets to his bedroom window five blocks away; it was more than that he could hear it, he could feel it moving through the neighborhoods, through the yards with their garbage cans and clothes lines and howling dogs, slipping through the gables of the abandoned church that he could see out his window, its crooked Greek cross shaking with the sound; he often imagined a monster appearing there (he'd just seen his first monster movie, *Gorgo*) taking the church down with its teeth and arms, its eyes now searching for someone, him, and then it was time to hide. The trains rolled through the center of the city, east and west, down the center of a street, 19th Street. On the north side a row of houses, houses like his, wooden, two stories, peaked attics, and porches—you could sit on your porch and watch the trains—the center of the black slums, and on the other side a graveyard that stretched for a mile, that lay seven blocks deep to the west; the wail of the trains passed from gravestone to gravestone, carrying on its back a thousand ghosts. This is what he heard.

He had a recurring dream, no, a nightmare, where the train and the monster became one; the black engine, its headlight a Cyclops eye, left the track to search for him; he hid in a cabinet beneath an arabesque buffet where his family kept a black Brownie camera; the space was too small yet he fit; there was no light, no window, yet he could see the black train stretching toward him with deadly intentionality. The meaning of this dream is all too obvious, but for the fact that a child shouldn't have a dream like this, but for its prescience, that he had it then so he could remember it now.

Later, much later, when he knew ghosts, he took a job collecting garbage in the middle of the night and rode the runner of a garbage truck outside the passenger door, holding onto the big rear view mirror with his gloved hands, the black night beating on him. They collected on 19th Street, from those homes facing the railroad tracks, facing the cemetery. Later still, in Salt Lake City, Diosa took an apartment across the street from a graveyard and he collected flowers from fresh graves for her mantle, a practice he stopped after the Night of Ghosts when one of her ex-lovers, long dead, brought her an armful of red gladiolas collected from a new grave. Against his blue Navy Flight uniform they seemed like blossoms of blood. He looked like a boy, the ghost, and he wept (though all the ghosts wept). "I can't see you," he wept, he whispered over and over. "But I see you," Diosa said. His unseeing eyes stared right at Roscoe, a line of cold, blindful sight. When Diosa's hand, reaching for the gladiolas, passed through him, the room burst into a heartache and for days after she slid through heartache like a scythe, the blood of the gladiolas a wake frothing with whispers. Roscoe wouldn't have thought he'd find that attractive, but he did.

From his father, who'd been a sniper in the Marines, Roscoe inherited a good eye. When he first held a rifle, even without a scope, through the V of the sighting device he felt as if he were touching the target, fifty yards away, with the tip of the gun barrel—exhale, squeeze, bull's eye. Then, with a second rifle, when he missed consecutively to the upper left, he handed the gun to the shooting instructor. "The sight is off," he said. And he was right. He was just a teenager then. Thirteen.

"Thought about the army?" said the instructor, a chiseled man, not tall, his black baseball cap said ARMY on it in white.

"My father fought the Japanese," said Roscoe.

"Koreans," said the instructor. "And Chinese."

"I don't want to shoot Vietnamese."

"Nobody wants to shoot anybody," said the instructor.

But Roscoe doubted that very much. It was the road not taken, that's what he thought. But you couldn't shoot all the Asians even some of the time or even some of the Asians all the time. He remembered falsely, or maybe from another life, coming home from war, and that time raising the rifle, adjusting for the faulty sight, and putting a bullet through the instructor's heart, though the bullet was intended for someone else, in fact, for a lot of other people. So much for intentions.

It wasn't that summer, though he felt, now, that it was; but then, some time then, he loved a sweet blonde girl, his first love. For her he snuck from his backyard tent and at two in the morning walked the naked streets of his city to find her porch-camping with a friend on her front porch. They walked down the street. He kissed her. He held her hand. And then one day, as if gripped by a god, he became furious with the world and left her. He began playing basketball day and night. That was all he could do. He entered a tunnel of dribbling and shooting and drills. He wore weights on his ankles under his pants, squatted a thousand deep knee bends while squeezing rubber balls in his hands, and when he emerged, he could soar like the Monkey King, slamming the ball through the hoop; there, in that moment, the fury subsided, his heart quieted; he flew like a cat, sleeping in the air as he jumped. He could do anything with either hand. And now people, schools, wanted him. But he felt inexplicable. And so he fell in love. A man's love, not a boy's, violent and inexplicable. But not yet.

He came to believe later in life that a boy came to maturity at fifteen and became that man until death, unless visited by some avatar. In the tornado of his teens, it had been Ares or Shiva, the name didn't matter, and now someone else. (There were scholars who surmised that the ancient Greeks, the Greeks of the *Iliad*, believed that neither their thoughts nor emotions were their own, but things visited upon them by the gods and nymphs of love, jealousy, war, hate, fate—Paris' wild love, Achilles' rage—so responsibility was subtle stuff, as were their afterlives, cool, shading, aching, ambivalent, sorrowful, abandoned by the passions of the gods).

By nineteen he knew there were men six inches taller than him who could do everything he could do on the basketball floor. That six years of breathing fire could bring him only a few more and then he would end up on some sideline bossing boys, his livelihood dependent on children who lived in his dead dreams.

He picked up Thales, Anaximander, Anaximenes, Anaxagoras, Pythagoras, Parmenides, Heraclitus, Leucippus, Democritus, and Empedocles, returned to Heraclitus and again settled on fire. He went on. He read everything. Marching in heaven on the hard thoughts of men who had lived in the clouds. The list alone would fill pages, a manly dance list of logic and detail gliding on the shadows of speculation. The sun yet rose and set.

He fell in love again, with a girl he remembered a thousand times, a girl with black hair and sad, dazzling blue eyes. More than anything it was the eyes. He couldn't think of her without pain and she took that pain in her thin hands and pulled it into her. She drove him to a cove on the peninsula that stretched like a bending arm from his small city. She left the road and drove into the woods, emerging on a beach. The beach was brown before a slate lake, the sky fraught with gray, big shouldered clouds; small white caps lapped the shore. He'd been on this peninsula hundreds of times and had never been here; no one he knew ever spoke of it; and there, alone, they undressed. She took his hand. Her black hair fell on her white, white shoulders. Her eyes became the lake and the sky. She cupped her hands and put water on his head and he remembered a story of his father skating across the bay, skating over the silver ice, a gift for Roscoe's mother, his body a miracle, a sacrifice, or was it Roscoe who did it, or would he do it in the future or before he or his father or this girl were ever conceived.

The girl was golden and he was blue.

"There," she said to him, her hands sliding from his cheeks, to his shoulders, his chest. "I cannot love you. This is not my heart, my skin. My life is on loan from a shadow. And you will be a virgin if you make love a hundred times, a thousand times."

His penis rose to her and she floated to him, placing him inside her. "A virgin" she whispered, her breasts upon his.

Was she a goddess, his first love, a dream, a memory from another life? Now he remembers lifting Diosa on the shore of the same lake on their wedding day, the sky rolling like a wrinkled blanket, the waves rising, her golden flesh pours into him and she laughs, "Do you remember when you carried me across the river?"

"It was so cold," he said, "my skin turned blue."

"Do you remember how you did it each time? A thousand times? Will you remember next time?"

But if he remembered it a thousand times would it be true?

The girl in the cove moved to Saratoga, New York or Sarasota, Florida. She became a macramé artist, then a horse trainer, then a journalist, and then a priestess. And now comes the moment when Roscoe first remembers her again, on the back of his thoroughbred mare who has spooked in the woods, torn the reins from her headstall and bolted for home; he hugs her foaming neck, the woods around him invisible inside her speed; his lungs burned with cold fire, and then he remembered the lake, the girl, her eyes.

In the years before the horse but after the girl, in Saskatchewan, somewhere east of Regina, lying on his belly on the seat of his motorcycle, throttle to the bar at 110 mph, she appeared next to him, straddling a white Moto Guzzi, black hair streaming from her helmet, a crooked grin. They pitched his tent alone on the plains, watching the sunset over a patch of trees, or is it a cloud, because he hasn't seen a tree all day, only wave upon wave of golden wheat. It was 11 pm and still light. He opened a bottle of red, Yugoslavian wine. He was married, divorced, running away, but he didn't know what he was running from.

If Zeno held that the distance between any two objects or locations to be infinitely divisible and thus illusory, then Roscoe wanted to run infinitely in that illusion; if for Heraclitus the cosmos was suspended like the tension of a drawn bow, then he wanted to live on the tip of that arrow; he was on a motorcycle sprinting from a coast, San Francisco to Vancouver, then east, east until the land ended. That night he dreamt of the girl lying next to him; she is a young woman now and he feels her dreaming her love at him and he wants to tell her that dreams don't last, they change direction, they become other dreams, and then in his dream he dreams of her as memory from a week ago in the Canadian Rockies; she came to him then, too, alone in the mountains at his campfire, and she asked him, "Do you wonder who I am?"

"A memory," he said.

"What else?"

"A future life absurdly lived."

He'd been writing a post card to his ex-wife. "I am here alone," he wrote and immediately as he wrote it, it became a lie, which is what things become when you write them down. On the front of the card, a photo of gray razor peaks against a blue sky; years later he'd remember that post card as he stared north to Mount Everest from the Tiger's Nest outside Darjeeling; the Himalayas hung above him in the sky, higher than heaven, blazing white, whiter than quiet or joy or oblivion, and he felt a tunnel inside himself and he wanted to hide there but he didn't know why; now he knows. He isn't dreaming anymore, and the girl, her black hair falling onto her shoulders and her eyes bluer than the sky on his post card says, the girl says, "You must do something for me because I'm falling in love." But with what? with who?

A white van pulls off the side of the road. A man gets out. He walks over and sits with them on the ground, folding one leg over another. Roscoe can't sit like that. After years of practice the best he can muster is a half lotus. Is it the light? The darkness? Roscoe can't tell if the man is old or young; he's pallid with a wispy, thin beard and his eyes are vague.

"I am," said the man. "I am."

"Who am?" said Roscoe.

"I am hungry," he said. "I'm the devil and I'm always hungry."

"Hungry as the devil," Roscoe said.

The girl touched Roscoe's wrist. "Don't feed him," she said.

But Roscoe put a hot dog on a stick and handed the stick to him. He poured him a cup of wine, emptying the bottle.

"Don't worry," the man who called himself the devil said.

But Roscoe remembered riding into battle in a pick-up truck, his rifle out the passenger window and Krishna at the wheel chanting that it didn't matter who they killed, everyone must die, everyone must return, he realized then that it didn't matter whether you worried or not, it didn't matter what you worried about, you couldn't get ready, not even for the inevitable. Getting ready changed nothing.

The devil roasted and ate the hot dog off the point of the stick, off the point of Heraclitus' arrow? The wine bottle refilled.

"We could do this all night," the devil said.

But they didn't. The man who called himself the devil got up and went into the back of his van.

Roscoe fingered the wine bottle. He poured a little. Sipped it. "This Yugoslavian wine is remarkably persistent," he said. "Is Transylvania in Yugoslavia?"

The girl, he's thinking now that her name was Naomi, put her hand over the top of his cup. "Don't drink it," she said.

"Romania," said Roscoe.

"You'll be forever dying," Naomi said.

So Roscoe filled his cup and drank deeply. "Living," he said. "Then dying."

"Then dying," said Naomi. "And dying. We need to do something about him," Naomi said.

"The devil?" said Roscoe.

He thought it odd, yet of course it was odd, running into the devil in British Columbia, and this girl, Naomi—was she his traveling companion?—should he make love to her?—though the man hadn't said he was Satan or Lucifer; maybe he was simply a devil, a minion, or maybe a man who had truthfully or mistakenly found inside himself the devil that is in all of us when others found God in all of us and yet others found neither or both. He gazed at the fire, wondering what fire was. What space did fire occupy, the poetry of gas and matter, heat and light, the miracle that made culture, that like Shiva sustained and destroyed. The girl now held a small revolver—he guessed it to be a .22—she'd have to get pretty close to the devil to kill him with that, besides, he didn't believe in devils or ghosts though he seemed to encounter them everywhere; he didn't have an ontology for either one, and he felt then, as he had ten thousand times, or he would feel ten thousand times more, that inside himself, if such an absurd phrase or space could be taken seriously, as if the self existed and had an inside and an outside, inside him lay nothing and everything, God, an angel, a whisper. The girl pointed the gun at him. "Do you want to go to Quebec?" he said.

Now he's on the runner of a dump truck. He will write a book about it. The teenager hanging onto the outside mirror started a waste

management company. He invented a fleet of mechanized compressors
run by one driver, then he transformed the trucks into robotic drones
run by fleet captains in a computer lab. Soon he no longer needed
the captains at all, only computers, and soon the garbage robots ran
themselves. They ventured into space. Encountered other worlds. But on
the bumper of the garbage truck the December wind is black and cold.
They cross the railroad tracks and turn onto 19th Street. A train howls
and he sees the singular headlight in the distance and across the way, in
the graveyard, he sees thirteen crows or one crow and twelve shadows,
and he can't tell whether the gray forms rising from the graves are ghosts
or mist, and he couldn't know, none of us do, that his life would pass in
front of his eyes like a breath, quicker than the chatter of his teeth in his
skull; the train rumbled toward and between the houses and the graveyard
in the middle of the night; Roscoe stepped from the bumper of the truck
and onto the tracks. He turned and faced the train, its mystical horn
now wailing. Across the way he sees himself hiding behind a gravestone.
Something in the future grips his heart. He turns his back and spreads his
arms as the train passes through him like a stiff wind.

He's driving his motorcycle through Manitoba with the girl whose
name is Naomi or Anne or Rebecca or Donna. Naomi. They've crossed
the plains and reached Portage La Prairie as a storm hits and night falls.
A white van begins to tail them and not until that moment does he feel
as if the truck has followed them just beyond his sight since that night
in the mountains outside Vancouver. The van flashes its lights that
seem to dance in front of them across the wall of rain. Roscoe signals to
the girl to pull off the road, he glides to her left to shield her from the
oncoming truck, but as he does the van is on him and swerves into him,
knocking him aside. As he lays his bike down, sliding onto the berm,

the van puts a bumper into the back tire of the girl's bike, pushing her forward. She goes down and the truck rolls over her, right front tire, then back. The van raises up on its left wheels, then lands. Through the black rain he sees the pallid face on the other side of the campfire.

The road is desolate. It's 1981 and there are no cell phones. The rain falls like lead. The girl has no pulse. He lifts his bike and drives to the closest farmhouse. There, a middle aged man with thinning red hair calls the police and an ambulance and he drives Roscoe in his pick-up to meet the authorities at the scene, but when they arrive there is nothing there at all.

DIOSA AND SWIFT MOVED to downtown Richmond. Statues of Southern generals on horses. People pronounced the Civil War the "silver wall" or called it the War of Northern Aggression. The maids were black, the servants were black, the janitors were black. She worked as a secretary for the Virginia State Police and was fired for spending their yearly food budget on two truckloads of Fruit Loops. Diosa changed her name to Lisa Diosa Swift. Then she dropped the Lisa. Jonathan Chrisman Swift changed his name to Swift Chrisman. That should have told her something, but she was young and wanted to be married. She dropped the Swift.

Swift Chrisman was a thinker and quite a drinker. He rebuilt his 1961 Austen-Healy 3000. He taught her martinis. She let him think that, rather than mention Sandy. Swift liked to wake up in the morning and start with a delicious booze milk shake. How healthy is that? Not very healthy, that's what Diosa said. Okay, Swift said, and started making booze fruit smoothies. Diosa accepted a fellowship from Valbuena to write poetry at UVA and began smoking Marlboros in the white pack; they called them Lights back then.

The sex wasn't great; the sex was barely sex; but he was cute and funny, witty as shit. He was thin. She should have figured something was wrong when he woke up early on Saturday mornings to wash his Austin-Healy. On Saturday, when you don't have kids, you lie in bed fucking all day, then wake up and go to dinner. His fascination with Rogers & Hammerstein, Andrew Lloyd Weber. Send in the clowns. He never pissed standing up. He never ate her out. He took a job with Swift Foods, his parents' corp., cut his hair and started wearing bowties again, this time with white shirts and dark suits. He wanted her to quit the MFA program and have some kids. He was hilarious at parties. He went broke buying booze and spent her asthma money on gin. She almost respected him for that, between gasps. But he could talk, he could banter, and he wasn't sexually dependent; it was kind of a pleasure not having to deal with it. She bought a vibrator.

We all go through our periods of uncertainty and self doubt, even Diosa. It was a time when she didn't understand that everyone wanted everything as easily as they could have it. That everyone was king or queen of themselves. That everyone had their reasons. That we were all businessmen. To think otherwise is to be a fool. To be otherwise, a martyr. To understand all of that, a poet. To deny all of that, something unimaginable, something she would love and never understand, never name. And was it not the poet's job to give words to the unspeakable?

They threw a Christmas party and Swift disappeared. It was
something he always did, disappear in the middle of parties, slipping
out with a friend for a drink and smoke, watching the southern stars or
an unusual southern snow. But his time, her timer was on. This time,
like any good husband or wife or parent who'd been going along and
going along and telling herself not to put two and two together because
when you do, what do you have, four? Why bother? This time she was
going to find out what she didn't want to know and already knew. She
waited ten minutes, then went outside and found Swift in the snow, top
down in his Austin Healy 3000, blowing his best friend. So later that
night they had one of those fights. It wasn't sex, it was a blowjob. And
in the morning, over coffee and fruit boozies, one of those, you know,
conversations. He loved her. He wanted a conventional marriage. He
wanted a wife and kids. He wanted to become chancellor of a boys' prep
school. Right. That's where he belonged. He wanted to go to bars at
night and sing show tunes. He wanted to blow his friends. What's the
problem here?

Well, she hadn't been honest when she married him. He was cute
and single and he wasn't Mathieu Valbuena. He was a lot of fun and
if he wasn't sexual, well, he was sexy, and she figured he'd change. If
she had yet to comprehend that she was the most beautiful woman on
earth, a hard enough thing to acknowledge because it caused adoration
and fright, aggression and weak-kneed collapse (and given that our
selves are formed outside our skins, she had come to believe that she was
adored and frightening, alluring and aversive) she nonetheless possessed
enough confidence in herself, and confidence in men in general, to
believe that it would only be a matter of time before Swift lined up
psychologically behind his inevitable erection—even gay men found her

attractive, or so she thought, for in women the line between the body and the mind is thinner, even if it's myth—and Swift did come into line, he just stepped out sometimes, well, in fact, it had become obvious that he got out of line more and more, and aside from playing the glamorous, fast talking dame on his arm at parties, soon enough what lay ahead was long nights at home with babies while he was out at clubs and baths singing show tunes.

What was she thinking when she married him? She didn't have a fucking clue. Maybe she'd been impulsive. Maybe? He begged her not to leave him. He'd change. He'd stop blowing men. Did she believe that? Did it matter? That January the greatest living poet in America came to teach at the University of Virginia and the greatest living poet in America was neither weak-kneed nor frightened.

But the greatest living poet in America was unhappy. He wanted a son. Someone to grow up and be almost as great a living poet as he. And when he looked at his wife, Anyita, whom he once found young and beautiful, he saw a woman approaching middle age. He'd thought, when he divorced his first wife, an intellectual poet of some renown who then married and divorced another poet from the other coast, he thought then that he needed someone to anchor him, not a poet, not an intellectual, but someone who could make his home more comfortable, who would want his child and agree with him about food and wine, who would be there when he came home from writers' conferences, tired and bored from the suckling adoration of young poets and old poets and gay poets and girl poets, girl poets too many of whom were compromises, a warm body and not love, an adoring mind but not an interesting one, (he left them in his wake, in anguish, mad for him with

longing) another woman to avoid at another school in another city who
thought he loved her poetry and not her young flesh which, in fact,
he could barely love, he could barely rise to when the vodka martini's
were swilled and the wine done, the brandy sniffed, the names dropped,
and he, barely honored, not quite truly appreciated, his own damn
life nagging him like a bitch and eating away at the cave of nothing
he called his ego that stood between him and immanent annihilation,
what was an erection, then, to him, and what was it to them? nothing,
nothing more than the flag of *angst*, the list of those who lay with him
growing like the line of the dead; then he could come home, his New
York condo deftly appointed in autumnal textures by an eye, an eye, not
some gaping mind, some ambition, but someone who found the depth
of the moment in a fine *Penne alla Puttanesca*, a gentle *Montepulciano*,
Eggplant *Raita, Crostini, Spaghetti alla Bolognese*. If his depth was too
vast for simplicity, his wife could yet be simple. But in no time he was
yet childless and she was writing a cookbook with his former publisher,
Nicco D____ (an ugly old friend who fucked young poets like a
scythe); worst of all, Anyita now contemplated a career in psychiatry.
What could prompt that?

Stephen M____, America's greatest living poet, was still a handsome
man, with an aquiline nose and jutting jaw, a full head of grizzly gray
hair, twinkling, almost mischievous eyes, thin, wry lips that broke into a
disarming smile that might make you believe he wasn't nasty. He was tall
and slender, and still liked to play tennis if it were not for a degenerating
lower back and some tennis elbow. He was only forty-five. He wrote:

Here in the hollow space
I call myself

In the cave of my masterly
Emptiness
You walk inside me
Clutching at my dark
Shadows which are the shadows of nothing
Gray forms in gray air
I am the moonlight
Of a moonless night
You are the last breath
Of my entropy

Well, so what if his best work was behind him? The *New Yorker* never noticed. And when his protégé, Mathieu Valbuena, invited him to spend a semester at UVA, Stephen M_____ was looking for a new pot to pee in. Even so, on that hot autumn day in Charlottesville when the air hung like wet wash and the leaves of the maples hissed under the hizzing cicadas, the insides of the old English building sweating cold sweat and the faces of the young poets-to-be waiting for him to teach them, touch them, turn them into the poet celebrities of the next generation, Stephen M_____ stared out into the yellow fluorescence, last night's wine still ringing in his head; how he hated Valbuena; how Valbuena had failed him with his minimalist imagery like a tiny tattoo on a fat woman's back; you'd think that a man who shot his own brother would have more emptiness to offer; yet he took Valbuena's invitation, not knowing that Valbuena hated him, too, though if he did it was only faint praise, and it brought him there to sit in front of the girl who had stolen Valbuena's own soul and let him go on living (better to have fucked and died, than never fucked at all, to truly live in that hollow cave of self to which America's greatest living poet could only allude, if poetry gave itself the task of giving words to the unspeakable, now Valbuena was speechless); but he had set the horrible trap, for the girl who murdered a hundred men and saved his life by denying him, had saved his life by stealing his soul, would soon sit in front of the mentor who in the wake of his love making had left a trail of longing and madness.

Stephen M______ stared out with great fatigue. There was no one left inside him to write a poem. He was afraid he'd written the last of them. Society had slipped from the precipice of literacy and he was an island once discovered and now lost in the mist, his soul only the shadow of a soul, his life stiff, his dick soft. "None of you will ever be poets," he said to them. "You can't go to school to become a poet. Go get jobs."

They sat silently before him. He surveyed them. There was one woman who looked like she could have been Miss Texas, with black night hair and a wedding ring, and another in a long coat with eyes like sapphires. She had a wedding ring, too. It was better if they were married.

"Can anyone here recite a line of poetry?" said Stephen M______. "Anyone?" he said to the silence. "Anything?"

And Diosa began chanting *Beowulf* in Old English.

"All right," the great poet said.

After five minutes of Chaucer in Middle English he stopped her again. He stopped her after six Shakespeare sonnets and Macbeth's soliloquy, ten minutes of *Song of My Self,* Ginsberg's "A Supermarket in California," some Merwin, some Levine. He put up his hand.

"Here in this hollow place," she said.

And Stephen M______, the greatest living poet in America had fallen in love.

Diosita: Is that how I would call you my little goddess? There were moments when I lay with you, on the verge of something momentous, my emptiness clambering across your softness, you full and young in the spots where I am empty and old; and then I think, yes, I have encountered life again, again if ever, and likely for the last time; to be inspired for the last time; the very last time; how many times can we die? Over and over. We die many more times than we live. But I am remembering you in that soft light, your breast in my hand; the hand that has written the silver of my lips, my lips, which have spoken the words that have broken the world apart; those lips touched yours. Now my wife wants the child she can't give me. You must save me from family life. Come to me. Break up my marriage. We will go to Italy. I will make you famous. Love, Stephen.

She thought hard about breaking up the marriage of America's greatest living poet. She'd met the wife, Anyita, and liked her; a quiet woman with intelligent and determined eyes; and why shouldn't or couldn't she have a child? Then there was Stephen M______ himself, statuesque, silver, a man for whom the poetry world lay like the Nile before the pharaoh. What do you think about riding in that boat, Cleopatra? Whose head will roll? Was it up to her? She lay upon her bed at night when her husband, Swift, was out somewhere, somewhere, and thought about herself. In the beginning and the end, what was the difference between her and the carnage of girl poets in the great poet's wake? Well, she was a poet, foremost, and he loved her work, loved her work as she recited for him in his silken bed like Sheherazade and he lay beside her enchanted and limp; if men rose to her like lightning, then from this man, America's first poet, whose reputation lay on the lips of girl poets like the dew of cum, his heart rose; his mind rose; he lay on his back, his tears streaming down his cheeks. "I have fallen," he whispered. "I have fallen." And just as well, for one thing to consider was if she fucked him and left him, he would, by the odds of her history, soon be dead. But did she really know that?

She joined him in New York. (Wouldn't everyone in the world now know, everyone in the world that counted, the world of sixty thousand American poets, wouldn't they know that she was with him in New York; sitting together in the lobby of Knopf, holding hands, planning lunch—that little Italian place in the Village, just off Houston, what's its name? they had a sensational wine list; there was a Chateau Neuf du Pape for only $400 that changed smells and flavors five times with every sip, from grape to raspberry, raspberry to a hint of melon, from melon to oak, oak to pomegranate—wouldn't they know?).

There, he sloshed his wine around the bottom of his large, tulip-shaped glass, smelled it. He snorted at the cork. He sipped. It needed a little air. A wine like this always did. "I will make you the queen of poetry," he said.

"What do you think," she said, "I was born yesterday?"

"Yes," he said, "that's what I think. And I think I was born the day before yesterday."

"You make me feel," she sang, "you make me feel, you make me feel like I was born yesterday."

"Yes," he said, "that's right."

"I am already the Goddess of poetry."

"No one knows," he said.

"What if everyone thought you the greatest of poets," she said, "even you, but you really weren't any good. At the moment of death, would you realize it?"

"What would it matter?"

"Because you would live in hell," she said.

"Only if you realized it," said America's greatest living poet. He sipped again. "Better," he said. "Try it."

The wine exploded across her tongue, slid silkenly to her palate, opened up at the back of her throat, filled her nose with ruby. How long could you live like this? How long before the days fell like funnel cakes and even this became bitter.

"You would spend eternity thinking hell was heaven," he said.

"Don't you want to change the world?" she said.

"Don't be silly."

"With your work."

"You're so young," said the great poet. "No one cares. Nothing would change if they did." He sipped his wine. She was the most beautiful girl he'd ever known. He tried, at that moment, to remember his best bottle of wine. Surely it was in France. Though there was a Zinfandel, from Napa, which shocked him, and a *Montepuccianno* in Tuscany.

Yes, the wine was good, but already, without knowing it, she had her first inkling that when a poet's heart moved to fine wine, his mind had been in the cellar too long. She'd fallen in love with him. Here, in the first breath of love, lay the first death of love. But even if you knew it, its signs were unreadable. His best days were behind him. He feared it. She knew it. They both, then, had too much at stake to do anything but deny it. That she inspired him now, he saw as a moment, maybe the moment of his rebirth—how can you ever know how long or for sure?—but he was falling in love, falling in love, his heart was filling with it and his mind was cloudy from it, even though he knew, he lied to himself in that moment, but he knew, that they wanted, they all wanted, even this young goddess, they wanted to be as great as you, equal to you; they wanted you to raise them up and it could not be done, and you had to move on before they asked; but then, maybe this time it would be different.

"Diosa Swift. Swift Diosa," he pondered. "Diosa M______."

"He's Chrisman now," she said, "But I'm not taking on any more names."

Yet he was a poet and a poet must be in love, or be torn by love, or have love torn from him or out of him; it must be tumultuous and fragile, frightening, horrible, brave; the back of time must crack on the forever of it and infinity fill the frail lie of his kiss; how could anyone, how could anyone else understand. The wind blew through the tunnel of skyscrapers as they walked the streets of midtown. He brought her to him. Kissed her there on Fifth Avenue. He was tall and even in heels she had to reach for his lips on her toes. His hand was huge and confident, holding the back of her neck, bending back her small head. If this is how it could be. If this is how it could be. Then why not?

Back in Virginia, her advisor, the poet Mathieu Valbuena, brought her into his office and wept.

(Why must she have this affect on men?)

"You're with him," he said. "He's stolen you from me."

(Why must it always be about possession?)

"He's ended my career. He's told the world that I'm a whelp, washed up."

"Are you?" she said.

"Yes," said Valbuena. He put his head in his hands. "Yes."

She unwrapped the scarf from her hair. She'd let her hair grow again, straight, to her shoulders, and dyed it yellow with black tips, which fell now on her neck. She took Valbuena's hands and wrapped the scarf around them, then sat down. She took out her pen.

> Darling, the black swans are rattling
> and your black bones click I'm wondering
> what we might do here in paradise without
> each other here to pick our teeth
> with the feathers of the dead we, oh we,
> oh yes, we might end up in bed.

"He will annihilate you," Valbuena said.

The greatest living poet in America moved to Utah. Lisa Diosa divorced Swift Chrisman. Swift got a great lawyer and took everything. She even ended up paying taxes on the money he stole from her. Death was too good for him, but she couldn't stop it from happening. On a business trip to New York, he caught his bowtie on a hook while exiting the Green Line on 59th. The doors closed and there he hung, outside the train, unable to step off or step back in, his eyes touching the eyes of the passengers on the platform; for a moment he spread his arms and legs out weakly, then whipped through the tunnel like a scarecrow; he was dismembered, pieces of him left hanging there at 68th Street. Diosa told herself the image was more disturbing than the death itself. Likely, he barely felt a thing.

AVATAR

WHEN ROSCOE'S PARENTS had two more sons they moved the boys, four of them, to the bedroom at the front of the house; two bunk beds, no closet, no electrical outlet, a single light bulb on the wall; the upstairs had an unfinished, ragged wood floor and no heat. His two sisters, in the bedroom next door, had a closet. His mother believed in God and died young.

Still a child, he awoke one night, sleepless, and finding more demons behind his eyes than in front of them, got up and went to the big window that overlooked the porch roof and the sidewalk and the street. Though inside the predawn light lay gray over his sleeping brothers, outside, under the huge arms of a spreading maple, people walked, no, paraded on the sidewalk. They wore hats, used canes, and pushed big-wheeled old-fashioned baby carriages. He didn't recognize anyone but he recognized one of the canes, a kind of carved, blond stick. There was one just like it in the toy shed attached to the kitchen at the back of the house, stacked in a box in the corner with the baseball bats and wooden swords. It was inscribed at the top near the carved handle with a name, Ellenberg, and a date, 1883. In a moment he knew what he would find out for certain later, that his house was built in the late 19th century along with four other houses that sat side by side, each house laid out the same, that Ellenberg had lived in his house, that the babies in the carriages in front of him, whether they had lived in the neighborhood at the time or not, were the parents of his neighbors parents, that the man below him, in a tweed coat and sporting cap, a thick red mustache, was Ellenberg, who stopped beneath the tree, turned to the window and raised the handle of his cane to Roscoe's eyes, It said, *Ellenberg 1883*. And then Ellenberg looked at him. Inside his blazing green eyes Roscoe saw a young woman, and a town, or felt a town, somewhere on the border of Germany or Poland, he felt it like those cities in your dreams that come to you with details and histories and memories you never had but for the times you return there in your dreams; he thinks Prussia, a place he'd never heard of and now didn't exist; all the lives there, what happened to them? whose dreams were they in now? his, and in that moment, though still a child, he wanted to find the words for them, he wanted to find the words that spoke deeper than words to the essence of each human being, ever deeper, to the essence of every animal, plant, and tree, every memory, every dream, disease, and desire; he would spend his life doing this without knowing he was doing it; there, at the window, though just a boy, he felt his first despair, prescient in that he would forget this vision in front of his home for sixty years and then, with his life growing behind him and shrinking ahead, he would remember himself as a boy looking into Ellenberg's dream of a town in Prussia and he, Roscoe, a boy, now dreamt of a girl there, and another girl unborn to people yet unborn; he knew must find her to teach him the words. In the meantime he would wade through humanity like Vishnu through soma, like a scythe through butter, like fire; his passion eating him inside out and outside in, even after he'd forgotten it all, and even later, when it fell upon him in longing, that it might not matter at all and yet meant everything whether it mattered or not.

Later, when Roscoe imagined destiny he pictured himself walking backwards, staring at the indiscernible past, moving blindly into the certain future. It wasn't that everything happened for a reason but more that each thing happened for many reasons, and what was a reason but some other thing, and soon reasons and things were proliferating like Hindu Gods; this was the rub of causality once you let it out of Occam's box. And if time and space were inseparable, then everything was implicated all the time, whether you went backwards or forwards, everything, always completely interdependent. But where was the ghost in that machine? Fate was personal, causality was not. Is that Buddhism? The Tibetans likened the soul, or better the no-soul, to fire, passed from one wick, one life, to the next, burning desire with no memory, buffeted by causes myriad and moral. Wanting to find something essential in that fire made him a Western man, and so he was whether he liked it or not. The mind was a terrible thing. And so he drove onward, walking backward, spying for the future in the past, the inevitable inside the uncertain—was it inevitable?—and then, on his motorcycle, diving toward some coast, the ghost pursuing him could not be killed by the demons pursuing her, that she was a million ghosts and he a million demons because, like dreams, the million ghosts and million demons have just one embodiment at a time, be they wish or dream or fear or fire; Roscoe was slouching toward the golden unknown, raging toward it, and she who he was raging toward, as we have seen, was the queen of too many men's fates. So if not for Diosa, Roscoe, yet unbeknownst to him, could neither live nor love nor die; he wouldn't exist.

In some distant future, in one embodiment of his fire, he stands in Brompton Cemetery in South Kensington, London, on a warm, warm late October day. There are dog walkers. Children chase squirrels, hopping between graves. A young woman in a bikini stretches out on a long, flat tomb. But for a fenced-off military section filled with the dead of World War One (the British lost thousands more lives in World War One than in World War Two) most graves in Brompton date from the mid to late Nineteenth Century. This cemetery sits close to Roscoe's flat on Finnborough Road where he awakens in the middle of the night absorbed by fright, reads Blake and watches the first passengers of dawn atop double decker busses flood by his window. He visits High Gate, East and West, (Communist intellectuals have paid to be buried near the grave of Marx), Bunhill Fields (a monument to Blake, but his grave is fenced off), Abney Park, unkempt, tree roots toppling gravestones and opening crypts, limbs form dark tunnels over the narrow grave paths; at the center a crumbling ghost chapel, its windows glassless and dead.

In Brompton, stretching north toward Fulham Street, there's a colonnade leading to a chapel, and beneath it catacombs. Its northwest corner sits beneath Stamford Bridge, where Chelsea plays football. East, on Brompton Road, Earls Court, once a scene for London's gays, and just west, a small train station where you can catch the tube, or surface trains out of London, you can see the walls of the cemetery from the train platform. Yes, graves and trains.

He thinks of the Howrah Train Terminal just across the Hugli-Ganges from Kolkata, the steaming river of humanity over and under the bridge, the water buffalo meandering near the river, then body upon body in the station; a parade of men carrying cadavers on stretchers, bodies to be transported to Varanasi to be incinerated and dumped in the Ganges; they will ride third class with him; he'll go to the burning ghats and watch. A family pays for the train ride and wood, but if the wood runs out the body is dumped regardless of whether it has turned to ashes or not. He swims there. A dead baby floats by. Then to Delhi, and Old Delhi, a city buried on itself nine times, and in Old Delhi the Red Fort, the place where the first Indian Revolt ended.

He doesn't even know what he's looking for, so when he finds Ellenberg's grave in Brompton it's on a path he walked a hundred times and yet he didn't see it, a brown stone beneath a Victorian shrouded urn. But this Ellenberg was a colonel who fought for the British in the Crimean War, then afterwards was sent to India where he died in 1857 during the first week of the rebellion. It was believed that his family, a wife, a daughter, and two sons, who followed him there, were murdered then, too, as were the families of many of the colonists in the first days. Those bodies weren't found, but some of the dead officers, at the end of it all, were shipped back and buried in England.

But one son, Sedgwick Ellenberg, escaped the massacre. He was found in a hole, badly injured and starved, beneath a burned out house, by a kindly Imam who hid him and nursed him back to moderate health, and then for the boy's safety and the safety of his own family, sold him to some itinerant merchants who were heading west. The young Ellenberg made due packing and unpacking camels and mules across the Punjab, Afghanistan, and Persia where the British were mopping up yet another war. There, in Tehran, was where he heard the legend of a woman so beautiful that no man, nor woman for that matter if she were so inclined, could gaze at her without falling hopelessly in love, but if he was fascinating enough to woo her interest and consummate his love he would, when she abandoned him, meet his untimely death. Ellenberg was a little young and a bit over-enslaved at the time to be greatly affected by the story, but some words made wonder get stuck to him, get stuck inside him—*houri* and avatar—and he recalled a legend he'd heard during his brief stay in India, from a story teller who set up to tell his tales next to the main fountain inside the Red Fort, of a golden reincarnated goddess, but if he recalled the fountain and the fort he yet couldn't remember the story.

It was in Tehran, where the British had re-instated a Persian ruler sympathetic to the Empire's terms of commerce, that Ellenberg located the British embassy and made his escape.

There are a number of ways to get to London from Tehran, but recalling the arduous voyage he'd recently taken with his mother and siblings around the horn of Africa in order to join his father in Delhi, where within months his family was massacred, he attached himself as a groom to an English supply train and worked his way by land, in a ironic reversal of his father's footsteps, through eastern Turkey, along the Black Sea and across the Straits of Kerch and into Crimea, then into central Europe, travelling along the eastern edge of the Carpathian Mountains. As he went, when his party camped and traded for supplies, he began to mingle with the locals, and because the Empire was everywhere, either by conquest or trade, there was always someone who spoke some English and could translate the stories, one of which, he always found, was of a woman, an avatar, who altered the lives of men, and sometimes even gods and monsters, by shattering them with their own passion: Sita, Helen, Cleopatra among others, and as he came into manhood his own passion arose for her, in each and any of her reincarnations, and this passion became a quest. He didn't know what he'd do if he found her, saw her, but to fall hopelessly in love and then, like the others, heart burning, die, which, of course, he didn't get to do, not like that, but as he fell into a Werther-like despair over his unrequited longing he did, one morning, outside a village with an unpronounceable name somewhere in the indefinable country of Prussia, spot a girl kneeling by a stream. Her hair fell on her shoulders and the light shimmered upon it in such a way that its color danced indescribably, and when she sensed him behind her she turned and captured him with her tortured eyes, eyes so blue that he fell into them and could see nothing else. She spoke, her voice like the black silk behind the stars. "What have I done?" she said. "What have I done but envy the dead?" And then she was gone.

It was a moment that could bring a life to tumult, bring it together or tear it apart. But Ellenberg wasn't Rama, Paris, or Caesar. His quest ended, he was simply quietly, quietly destroyed.

He returned to England where he inherited his family's small estate. At maturity he joined the military until in 1883, at the Battle of Tel el Kabir in Egypt, his right leg was severely wounded, thus the blond cane, made of ash, *Ellenberg 1883*. Back in London he hooked up with a ship building company that eventually led him to establish a branch in the States on Lake Erie where he fell in love with the long, red sunsets over the lake when it wasn't snowing or raining, of which it did much, but only made the few sun-full days and bleeding sunsets more special, each time the blue of daylight died in the splay of light and then into darkness.

He never married. He couldn't. Of course, you know why, but he didn't know; things so deep must be forgotten. The vision of the girl outside the Prussian village dropped from his memory the way the jewel of the sun dropped into the lake. Sometimes survival, if we have that in us, is all we have left in us. Until one night some years after he died, he joined a parade of ghosts, something ghosts are apt to do if you know anything about them, and in front of the house where he once lived he spotted a boy in the window and then, for a moment, remembered, because ghosts themselves are not immortal, but momentary, and if their memories are eternal, they only come upon them in a flash, like touching fire; not until then, meeting the boy's eyes, did he remember the girl, and when the boy saw that memory inside him, the goddess danced between them. For the briefest sliver of infinity, she danced in Roscoe's heart, and then gone, gone from heart, from head, from memory. Ellenberg, the ghost, lifted his cane. Fate danced. We are helpless.

THE SILVER WALL

SHE WORKED FOR the Richmond Museum of the Civil War, archiving items in the basement. She ate lunch in the kitchen with the black help. In front of a mirror, she tried on Robert E. Lee's coat. He had quite a nice sword, too. In an old box she found a letter from Jefferson Davis to Colonel Edmund Brady, Commander of the Confederate Army of the New Mexico Territory, outlining plans to annex California and the New Mexico Territory and invade Mexico and Cuba, then expand the Confederacy to Central and South America. Everybody's got big, big plans. A man came into the office one day when she was the only one there. He was thin, with a dark, receding hairline, something grim with events to come in his brown eyes. "Is this the Museum of the Silver Wall?" he said. When he spoke, he barely opened his mouth, barely pronounced his consonants, and spoke so slowly that a train could pass between his words. She liked the music between those words.

"No," said Diosa, "that's down the street."

He was back in ten minutes. "You lied to me," he said. "This is the Silver Wall Museum."

"Do you want to see Robert E. Lee's coat?' she said.

"I want to see his horse," said the man.

"Traveler," she said.

"Is he stuffed like Trigger?"

"Not here he isn't," Diosa said.

"You're kind of cute for a weird girl," said the man.

"You're kind of cute for a cracker," said Diosa.

"Well, let's take a look at that coat," he said.

She led him down into the basement and over to a rack where she'd hung the coat after pulling it from a moth-balled trunk.

"Want to wear it?" said Diosa.

"No," he said, "you wear it." His accent was so musical you could almost smell it. And she knew where this would end up, don't you? But what's one redneck, more or less? She put on Robert E. Lee's coat and he came to her.

"What are you looking for here at the Silver Wall Museum?" she said.

"Nothing," he said. "I'm looking for the Richmond Bank. I was told it was near the Richmond Bank."

"Down the street the other way," she said. He wasn't that big, and he was quick, but he made a sound in his throat like you'd imagine a chorus of hummingbirds.

"Damn," he said, "I fucked Robert E. Lee's coat."

"And what's more," said Diosa.

"What's more?" he said.

"That's what's more," she said.

He went down the street and tried to rob the Richmond Bank where the Richmond Police shot him dead.

So she quit the Richmond Museum of the Silver Wall and that's when she went to work ordering provisions for the Virginia State Police.

"Stop working for the Virginia State Police," wrote Stephen M______. "Come to Utah where it never snows, except on the mountains. Why work? Be a poet. Scratch the blank soul of the empty world with your delicacy. Leave it wounded when you depart."

There was something fishy about all that, but she couldn't put her finger on it. And a big police officer was flirting with her. There was nowhere good that she could go. She ordered the truckloads of Fruit Loops, got fired, and ended up teaching outside Middleburg, Virginia, at the Foxcroft Preparatory School for Girls where, among others, she taught a young princess from Ghana. Indeed, there at Foxcroft, Diosa taught many princesses of potentates and dictators and deposed dictators where in the hills of Virginia they rode their hot blooded horses, experimented with lesbianism, sneaked off to D.C. to fuck the sons of senators, seethed in the decadence of southern decadence; that's what I like about the South.

Chaperoning one of those D.C. excursions, standing in front of a diorama of stuffed elk in the Natural History section of the Smithsonian Institute, Diosa met a scientist from Uruguay who survived the military dictatorship by teaching botany for free and obtaining a government license to beg in front of the cathedral in Montevideo. To be allowed to teach he had to prove he had no political history and lived without opinion. What they had in common: the morbid immortality of stuffed animals standing delicately poised on the cusp of the next moment; their teeth yellowing, their fur growing coarse, abandoned now by the site seekers of Animals Parks and Sea Worlds and giant zoos, the mystery of their once mysterious lives corrupted by television nature shows; there, so unconscious and fully loaded; the hand that stuffed them long dead; in the corner of the exhibit she spotted a live mouse. No one else there, just the poet and the scientist and the mouse, stuffed into a moment. That day she bought him lunch, but later he couldn't break the habit of begging, and singing songs for food, and came to her window where she threw him scraps of bread. Without thinking, or rather, thinking of the mouse and not the scientist, the night before winter break she descended from her window on a rope made of silk scarves and fucked him on the lawn. When she returned from vacation, he'd died of starvation. Who wouldn't?

Stephen M______, America's greatest living poet wrote her, "Come to Utah. Come to Utah where there is no winter and no summer. I will make you the Queen of Poetry." She was twenty-five. Queen of Poetry sounded pretty good. She filled out an application to the University of Utah, then threw it away. Maybe the greatest living poet in America could survive her. Then again, maybe no man could. Now she knew. She knew it was true. That breaking up is hard to do.

Diosa decided to drive to Salt Lake City and become the Queen of Poetry. Back then she met a woman named Karla who had four kids—an oldest daughter, Dawn; twins, Flora and Fauna, who did not look alike; and a son, Retro—each, but for the twins, had a different father, though they all had the same last name because Karla only married men named Kevorkian.

"You know," said Karla, "you get tired of changing your name."

"Don't I know it," Diosa said.

Retro's father was a famous wild game hunter and sport fisherman. Flora and Fauna's was a painter whose favorite subject was girls in long dresses on row boats in Southern swamps, and Dawn's a doctor who helped terminally ill people commit suicide so ended up in jail. Right then, Karla was seeing a Marxist architectural theorist named Schaffy Kevorkian who'd just taken a job at Cal Berkeley.

Diosa coached softball at the Foxcroft School for Girls. She won the Virginia State High School Softball Championship without knowing how to catch, hit, or throw, without knowing the rules, without really understanding what her players, who were all the daughters of Central and South American dictators, were saying. She had a baseball hat that said *Diosa* and before every game she held up a Magritte painting of a pipe that had *Ceci n'es pas un pipe* written under it. Then she held up a softball and said, "Recuerda, en realidad, esta polleta no es blanda." But it was time to move on.

At the moment she and Karla were sitting cross-legged in an alley off Monument Avenue in Richmond, Virginia behind their favorite thrift store; their long black coats fell around them like tipis; they drank from a wine bottle and shared a joint; snow fell. Then, Diosa was yet twenty-five years old, Karla Kevorkian forty.

"Queen of Poetry," Karla Kevorkian said. She blew smoke. "How many before you?"

Diosa sucked on the fifth of Gallo. "None after," she said.

"That's what they all say," said Kevorkian.

"He hasn't been king that long," said Diosa. She put out the roach. "I could move to Vermont and have Ruth Sparrow name me after a bird."

Karla Kevorkian brushed snow from Diosa's hair. "Snow in

Richmond," she said.

Diosa pulled out her Marlboros. "Want a cigarette?" she said. She lit for the two of them and they smoked. "It never snows in Salt Lake City," Diosa said.

"I get it," said Kevorkian.

Diosa offered her the wine bottle.

"Can't I get an Irish coffee somewhere around here?" said Karla Kevorkian.

"Not for free," said Diosa.

"How far is Salt Lake City from Berkeley?" asked Kevorkian.

"On the map?" said Diosa. She held up her free hand and separated her index finger slightly from her thumb.

"Six inches," Kevorkian said. A chick joke.

"Fifteen hours," said Diosa. "Day's drive."

"I lived in San Francisco in the Sixties," said Karla K. "That's where I met Dr. Kevorkian."

They sat for a moment, the snow falling.

"Fifteen hours is a nice distance from a man," Karla Kevorkian said.

"It never snows in Salt Lake City," Diosa said.

So Karla Kevorkian made arrangements to have her kids, who were all pretty little back then, shipped out to Salt Lake City after she found a home. Diosa lost everything in her divorce to Swift Chris; she even paid for his move to New York. She fucked her divorce lawyer who died a week later from a cocaine overdose. Though she was a surreal consciousness to whom causality was an anathema, there was something almost Pythagorean about her love life and she'd begun to sense it the way a fish feels another fish from ten feet away.

They piled what they could into the trunk and back seat and on top of Diosa's white 1969 BMW 2002—Snow White—and headed out.

"You have a map?" Karla Kevorkian said.

"It's out there somewhere," Diosa said. She wrote:

Touchstone: Another Digression

Truly, I would the gods had made thee
less poetical.

Or had given me a very beautiful poem
to give thee—

to use as a path, as it were, toward thee, my
beloved, and toward a vita nuova—

a poem which would be, would it not, a kind of
infinite metaphor for the phrase

I love you. And yet who is this I? Who is
this you? How shall we exorcise the

terrifying arbitrariness of our story?
I want you to exist in a body other than

the flesh and blood of my fingers lettering
you out, to be more in your life and death

than a great reckoning in a little tavern.

More than a quarrel over a bill—

I want and yet do not want
to be weaned from the full milk of the poem—

initiated into something more bitter
and divided. I would feign not feign

any of this. I would feign deign an actual
vacation with you and your little horse

in some fairy-tale forest of lions and palm
trees. There to be merry, if not married

inside the great, stubborn space of moving
sentence, enveloped in both longing and

myth, wearing the ritual skin of a stag
we have slain together. Let us leave

behind painted images of our hunt
which like a series of endlessly reflecting

mirrors might one day come to stand for
all hunting.

But it was not for Stephen M____.

ZEN BOWLING

"I'M IN LOVE with you," said the ghost, "and when I'm not in your thoughts, I don't exist. My non-existence bleeds from my eyes. That's what you see in front of you on the road as you fly into my nothingness. It's my wanting that pulls you forward, the wind behind you the wake of my longing."

He'd driven from Thunder Bay along the northern shore of Lake Superior to Sault Saint Marie where she'd met him on the road, her bike swinging in next to his (he was not surprised), then moving ahead, then falling back, the dance of motorcycles in a lane, the joy of head-snapping acceleration; he wasn't yet thirty. She was nineteen.

How did you die, Naomi?

I died when you rejected me. I starved myself. I dove headlong to the ground from the top of a tree. I sold my no-soul to the demon on my tail.

No, he said, you'll travel to Israel and marry.

In Israel I die under a bulldozer on the West Bank.

You get your Ph.D. there, at the Hebrew University. You marry. You have two children, a girl and a boy.

I sell this motorcycle for scrap metal.

You take a job at Berkeley.

In the tent she was naked in his lap.

I love you, she said. You ran away, but you are my vacant destiny.

And he had run away. And it wasn't the first time he'd been followed. When he was nineteen he met a young woman from Scranton, Pennsylvania, named Marianna Sappho with almond eyes and tan hair; she liked to make love in Catholic churches at night (she knew how to break into buildings—my other boyfriend, she said, is a cat burglar, a thief—behind altars, in sacristies, spreading priests' vestments across the floor like quilts, but she had a gentleness so deep it made him cry. She wiped his tears with her fingertips. I can't love you, he said, because love and God were torn from his guts a thousand times when he was twelve; of course, something like that you can't remember, so he lived like a page torn in half. Here, now, gentle reader, we must live in that gap, as Roscoe did for decades. Another story for another time.

I'll love you anyways, said Marianna Sappho, and one miraculous warm November day, after he'd bicycled to the peninsula for a swim, she sat waiting for him on the beach; in the arms of Indian Summer he sat down next to her.

"I'm pregnant," she said.

"Mine?"

"Maybe."

"Winter," he said. He didn't know why. "Winter is so soon."

"Everything is too soon," said Mariana Sappho. "Will you marry me?"

"I'm a garbage collector."

"The other guy's a criminal."

"I can't marry you," Roscoe said.

"Then make love to me now," said gentle Marianna. "Nothing matters. Make love to me now."

But a year later he married Carona Petras, a moving van heiress from Beaver Falls, a big mistake if you don't want to be followed. He mistook her for a hippie. Everybody mistook everybody for a hippie then. He was a vegetarian, so her father gave them a freezer full of beef. That's how that went. He left her and she followed him to Rudolph, a town of 300 in northwest Ohio, freezer and all, and while he tended a garden, made vegetable soup and baked loaves of whole wheat bread, waiting for the dough to rise he read Plato and Aristotle, Plotinus, Augustine, Maimonides, Boethius, Aquinas, Averroes, Anselm, Sigur. He read Bacon, Descartes, and Hobbes, Leibniz, Spinoza, Newton and Kepler, Berkeley and Hume, Kant, Hegel (Hegel was almost impenetrable so he picked up Coppleston), Nietzsche, Schiller and Schopenhauer. Then, finally, Wittgenstein, the *Tractatus* (and Max Black's *Guide*) and the *Investigations*. He read Americans: Thoreau and Emerson, Charles Sanders Peirce, William James, Howard George, Josiah Royce, John Dewey and George Herbert Mead, then back to Europe, Durkheim, Weber, and Marx, Freud and Jung, Bergson, Kierkegaard, Jaspers, Heidegger, Sartre, Simone de Beauvoir (a woman!). Back to Britain: Jeremy Bentham, John Stuart Mill, F. H. Bradley, G. E. Moore, Bertrand Russell, Alfred North Whitehead (even more dense than Hegel), J. L. Austin, A. J. Ayer, Anthony Flew and Thomas Kuhn, C. L. Lewis. He moved east, read the Vedas and Upanishads, the commentaries of Sankara, the works of Patanjali and Mahavira, the Buddhist sutras and Nargajuna's *Mulamadhyamikakarika*. On warm afternoons he rode an old Schwinn bicycle through the cornfields to a deep clear abandoned quarry where he lay on the jagged rocks and climbed into the trees and dove through the sky into the cold infinity of blue. Just like that.

Meanwhile, Carona had become a photographer and taken a job with a rock magazine in Toledo, *Exit*, funded by its publisher/editor, Alex Allen, an heir to the Firestone Tire corporation. Roscoe eked out a living borrowing Carona's car on weekends and delivering the magazine to bookstores and college campuses around eastern Indiana and western Ohio. And while he baked and gardened and souped and read, ignoring a freezer full of beef, he fell into a holy self, God blind, but holy, that imbued him with an unselfconscious, nascent, naïve sophistication, or sophisticated naiveté, a soft stubbornness and hard willingness which, as you see, is hard to describe, while Carona took photos and made love to other men, though she made love to him, as well, even if she recognized the indescribable change in him that made her uncontainably and frustratingly wild. But one night when she was out very late, he went into her darkroom and went through her photos, full body portraits of men, nice naked photo of Alex, and he bothered to figure it out. That night, or early morning, after she'd come to bed, he stole her car and headed west.

She packed up a moving van, found him in Albuquerque (how did she know?) and moved back in. She liked the security. This system works, she told him, because you would fall in love with someone else, but I won't. Well, it was working for her.

At the New Mexico State Fair he ran off with the Snake Girl and her python in her red 1960 Cadillac convertible—she was mostly too fucked up to do much driving; Roscoe liked driving and came to like heroin, too, but he was very disciplined—and drove that car all the way to San Francisco. But he couldn't afford San Francisco, or heroin, so he hitched east, got a staph infection from a hangnail and ended up in a medical clinic in Davis where, after some x-rays (why x-rays?) the doctor told him "You know, it's very strange, but your insides are bigger than your outside." He showed Roscoe his lung x-ray that was only partial. "I got your chest in the lens but your lungs don't fit on the negative."

"How big is my heart?" said Roscoe.

Yes, Roscoe, how big is your heart? Big enough to hold Diosa?

He crashed a party and met a gentle gay man named Buzz who offered him a room as barter for housekeeping. Roscoe learned to cook, not just bread and soup—Buzz liked turkeys! a long story—and Roscoe cooked for Buzz. Buzz's boyfriend was a rake and on the nights of his infidelities Buzz wept and Roscoe consoled him. Roscoe wasn't afraid of men.

Roscoe took a job as a landscaper's assistant, meaning he pulled weeds and mowed lawns, and saved up enough money to buy his motorcycle that he rode into the Rumsey Canyon foothills to eat mushrooms and commune in the fields with black bulls, lie on the black sand of streams and swim in the broad swimming holes of Rumsey Creek, lying naked on the warm, sandstone rocks mid-stream, or he drove to Berkeley or Santa Cruz to crash parties.

Sometimes he played basketball in the UCD gym where he was spotted by a junior administrator, Dandy Jones, who recruited him to play for the varsity basketball team.

"I don't want to play for a team," said Roscoe.

"You'll have to go to school. How about writing school?" said Dandy.

"Will I have to write something?" Roscoe said.

Dandy offered him a deeply administrative and practiced half-smile and half-frown, his brow furrowing slightly under his black-rimmed glasses. "I'm thinking of the university," Dandy said.

He dragged him to a local bar, the Pyramid, where the writing students hung out. Roscoe met poets: one gentle male poet, two lesbian poets, a bevy of women poets with searching eyes; and fiction writers: an Italian Fabulist short story writer, a southern short story writer from Brooklyn by way of Mississippi who didn't believe in racism or sexism, a novelist from Mississippi named Mississippi who had photos in his wallet of all twelve of his kids (this one here looks just like me, he said, the others look like my wife), a cowgirl novelist who was writing a novel about 19th century lesbian horseback riders in Hyde Park, a Vietnam vet Communist novelist who wrote about the war, and a mad man who wrote all kinds of poetry, short stories, novels, even plays in invisible ink who eschewed the difference between the blank page and the written page. They were all very suspicious of Roscoe.

In the meantime, Roscoe figured if he was going to be a writer he better read something. He went to see the visiting fiction writer, Bill Kittredge.

"Don't be a writer," said Bill Kittredge.

"I've barely written," said Roscoe.

"That's the best time to quit," said Bill Kittredge.

Roscoe visited the resident poet, Karl Shapiro.

"Don't be a writer," said the kindly, white-haired Karl Shapiro. "Especially, don't be a poet."

"What should I read?"

"Everything," said Karl Shapiro.

Roscoe started with the epics. He read *Gilgamesh* and *Beowulf,*

The Iliad, The Odyssey, The Aeneid, Ovid's *Metamorphoses, The Ramayana* and *The Mahabharata, The Bible, The Koran.* He read Dante and Milton, *The Song of Roland, The Niebelungenlied, Tristan and Isolde, Le Morte d' Arthur, Sir Gawain and the Green Knight,* then *Don Quixote.* He picked up an anthology of American Lit and read it cover to cover. When he encountered a fiction writer he read all their stuff: Cooper, Hawthorne, Melville, Poe, Sarah Orne Jewett, Kate Chopin, Charlotte Perkins Gillman. He read Crane and Norris, Dreiser and Twain (he loved Twain). Henry James (okay, not all of him) and William Dean Howells, Cather and Wharton, Sherwood Anderson, Dos Passos, Jack London, Fitzgerald, Hemingway. Faulkner, Flannery O'Conner, Carson McCullers. He read Kerouac and Burroughs, Margaret Atwood, Marge Piercy, Raymond Chandler, Dashiell Hammett, Fante, Updike, Malamud, Eldridge Cleaver, James Baldwin, Ishmael Reed, Paul Bowles, Saul Bellow, Alice Adams, Norman Mailer, even Gore Vidal. He read Hawkes, Barthelme, Coover, Gaddis, Barth, and especially William Gass. He read Chuck Kinder and, finally, Ray Carver and his University of Iowa acolytes. He found that poetry made him nervous, but he did read Walt Whitman, Emily Dickinson, Hart Crane, Sylvia Plath, Wallace Stevens and William Carlos Williams, Ginsberg, Corso, and Snyder, Adrienne Rich, Anne Sexton. Back to fiction he slid south to Paz and Fuentes, Borges, Cortazar, Allende, Marquez, Eduardo Galeno, Juan Rulfo, even Leonora Carrington. Now Europe: Voltaire, Balzac, Zola, Flaubert, Chekhov, Kafka, Tolstoy, Dostoyevsky, Sartre, Camus, Marguerite Duras, Bruno Schultz and, well, Stanislaw Lem. He read Sterne, Fielding, Richardson (not Trollope), Jane Austen, Emily and Charlotte Brontë, George Eliot, Mary Shelley, oh man! Mary Shelley! Arnold Bennett, Oscar Wilde, Virginia Woolf and Elizabeth Bowen,

Ford Maddox Ford, Jean Rhys, E. M. Foster, Evelyn Waugh, Summerset Maugham, Graham Green, Anthony Burgess, some Ezra Pound and T.S. Eliot. Well, he really couldn't read everything. He sat in on Sandra's Gilbert's Virginia Woolf seminar. Woolf lit him up. And across the back row of the classroom, in the opposite corner, sat a black-haired, wire-rimmed Hasidic Jewish intellectual named Naomi Weis. Once, after class, he gave her a ride home on his bike.

"What's your politics?" she shouted in his ear.

"Nihilist, anarchist, socialist," said Roscoe.

"That's ridiculous," said Naomi Weis.

"Like Trotsky," said Roscoe. "All politics are ridiculous. What do you want to be when you grow up?"

"I want to narrate my own suicide like Kate Chopin!" shouted Naomi. "That's why she's a better writer than Virginia Woolf."

"That's why Woolf is a better writer than Kate Chopin," said Roscoe. "She kept it to herself."

In front of her apartment she said, "I hate you. Kiss me."

"Never on the first date," Roscoe said.

That's how that went.

Roscoe read some playwrights: Aeschylus, Sophocles, Euripides, Aristophanes, Shakespeare, Beckett, Sartre, Ibsen, Pirandello, George Bernard Shaw, Arthur Miller, Eugene O'Neill, Lillian Hellman, Sam Shepard. More fiction: John Fowles. He read Calvino and Buzatti. He learned French and read Camus, Piaget, Derrida. He was doing mop up. He read *A Thousand Nights and One Night*. He imagined the work of Bolaño and Aira—he saw it coming. You might think this impossible, but he'd fallen into a hole of time, like a page in *To the Lighthouse*, or like *Orlando*, where his future was already and his past was his destiny, his life was like the galaxies at the edge of the universe moving faster than light and disappearing over the event horizon, authors and books floating by like the ships at the beginning of *The Iliad*. He'd begun reading the Romantic poets, Blake, Wordsworth, Shelley, Keats, Byron, then Carona showed up with her moving van. "How did you find me?" he said to her.

"How could I not find you?"

"Why are you following me?"

"I'm not following you. You're following me. You just got here before I did."

Given Roscoe's ontology that was hard to dispute.

Carona suggested he move in with her. She'd support him while he wrote a novel for his Master's thesis. That lasted about a month. "It doesn't matter," she said, "your dick is too fat." He moved back in with Buzz who gave him a copy of *The Tale of Genji*. "Life imitates art imitating life," Buzz said.

Buzz liked to throw huge parties for his gay friends and lesbian friends and undecided friends with their forlorn wives. Between those forlorn wives and the twenty-five women in the Virginia Woolf seminar and the deep eyed poets, Roscoe plowed a fertile field; if he could not fall in love, he yet found he loved women very much; he believed himself a failure if, after making love, his partner didn't look as if she were on the verge of death. Then there was Naomi Weis, who pushed against his chest with her palm as they made love. "Trains," she said to him, "graveyards and trains." How did she know? She was a ghost.

He spent some evenings with the fiction writers, snorting coke, smoking pot, popping valium and drinking whiskey. Dandy Jones dragged him to a basketball practice where he watched those lanky boys lunging and sweating. "They need a shooter," Dandy said to him. "You'll get an education."

"I already got one," said Roscoe. That night he went dancing with the Director of Creative Writing's girlfriend, didn't even kiss her, and got kicked out of the writing program before he even got in. Good thing he didn't write that novel. He headed for Berkeley, Naomi Weis, live and in person back then, on her new Honda Hawk hot on his heels. He found a party a couple blocks off Telegraph, entered, and ran into Marianna Sappho, a dark toddler in her arms. She wore her hair loosely fastened up, as Dante Gabriel Rossetti said, so that it fell in soft heavy wings. Her complexion looked as if a rose tint lay beneath her dark skin; her eyes were kind and golden brown.

"Darko Jr.," Marianna Sappho said, offering up the child.

"He doesn't look like me," said Roscoe. The child's dark hand grabbed Roscoe's index finger.

"He has your smile," said Marianna Sappho. She'd traveled west, looking for work. Darko, Sr. was in jail. "Train robbery," Marianna said. "Striking into new territory."

"Pretty old new territory," said Roscoe. "He should have read William James' train robbery argument in 'The Will to Believe.'"

"Would you like to make love?" said Marianna. "I have condoms."

"Fat condoms?"

"Fat condoms."

And Roscoe did make love to her because, well, he loved her in his way, and decades later still had a place in his heart for her, a gentle, deep-hearted woman with soft hands and a musical, lithe love, though Roscoe didn't make love to any woman who he couldn't at least imagine himself making love to again, and even again, which, in fact, he often did, sometimes for months or, off and on, even years; he just wanted nothing to do with monogamy.

In a dark room on a dark bed, Roscoe and Marianna made love, Marianna moan-humming some dark, unrecognizable melody, Darko Jr. playing quietly nearby with a couple of popsicle sticks.

When he left the party, Naomi Weis caught him outside. Nails in his chest she said, "I smell her on you."

Roscoe put his palm on her heart and headed for Oregon where she caught up with him in Medford as he napped in a park next to the Rogue River. Quick as a bunny she was on top of him.

"I don't orgasm," she said. "You should know."

"I don't either," said Roscoe.

"Death is the only orgasm," said Naomi.

"You're only nineteen," said Roscoe.

"You're only nineteen," said Naomi. Then she leapt from him, stepped back, put her feet in the river.

"Don't," said Roscoe. "The current is deceptive." He knew, because decades later he would almost be swept way in the Ganges, a death prevented only by its metaphorical heavy-handedness.

Naomi stepped into the brown, swirling current, went down. She came up, gasped. "I'm narrating my suicide," she choked. "Glub, glub," and was carried away by the current, under a bridge, under a canopy of green trees.

Back in Davis, a poet he was seeing, Dianna Trix, was leaving for Vermont to live with Ruth Sparrow.

"Don't do it," Roscoe said to her, because he'd been sleeping inside the poetry world and knew plenty about it. "She'll put you in a cage and name you after a bird."

"I'll be different," said Dianna Trix.

"That's what they all say," Roscoe said, and of course he was right. Anything that happens once has probably happened before and will happen again, and again, even if you can't step in the same river twice.

He picked up some teaching when the Communist Vietnam vet, Cookie Duncan, let him teach his fiction writing class. Duncan's coke dealer was a Division Two All-American wide receiver on the UCD football team who bribed the registrar to enroll all the football players in the course. Duncan traded them grades for coke, paid Roscoe with the money from his fellowship. So it was kind of already in the bag, all Roscoe had to do was show up, though a lot of football players showed up, too, and tried to learn how to write from Roscoe who admittedly knew very little about it. Duncan was an odd Communist, but as he said, it was hard to be a Communist in America. Next quarter it was the basketball team.

"Hey, I know you guys," said Roscoe.

"You're not Cookie Duncan," said the shooting guard that Roscoe would have replaced.

"I'm not dunkin', I'm teachin', said Roscoe, and indeed he hadn't dunked in a few years.

"Are you getting the coke?"

"Cookie gets the coke," Roscoe said. "I get the windrush of sated pedagogy."

When the class emptied, the only woman enrolled, Anna Hornikova, walked up and lifted his bowling shirt that said *Suzuki* on the pocket. "Who's that?" she said.

"My favorite Zen bowler," said Roscoe, and it was half true.

Anna Hornikova put her finger on the muscle that ran from his stomach through his groin. "I want that," Anna Hornikova said.

Right then Roscoe knew it was time to get out of town. But you don't always do what you know you should do.

Anna Hornikova had a way of looking at you that said what you were thinking and her answer was usually yes. She was the mistress of several European and South American sports stars, at least according to her roommate, Serum Prajapati, a dark, mystic snake charmer and pigeon trainer. When Roscoe wondered how two people so young could be so well travelled and sophisticated, Anna answered, "Wealth."

"You are opposites," said Serum, wrapping a python around them as Anna rocked on Roscoe's lap in the middle of Serum's giant waterbed, "Shiva and Kali, destructive innocence, finally tuned passion like the string of a bow."

Those aren't opposites, thought Roscoe.

"Oppositions held in tension," moaned Anna Hornikova, and of course that explained everything. In the future, his daughter, Marlena Dali, wraps a python around herself in Melbourne, dances on stilts, swallows swords and breathes fire. She tells her raging audience, I am creating my father. Half a world away he stands with Diosa in the SS. Mary and John Victorian graveyard on Cowley Road in Oxford, England, before the headstone of lovers long dead. Diosa sings softly, "Miss Otis Regrets" (you know the words, don't you?). Love will not survive the grave. Outside his bathroom window in The Queen's College, across an alley, atop a fourteen-foot wall, weeds spring from the cracks of the bricks, they sprout with yellow flowers. Anna Hornikova's erect nipples slide against his own. "I don't orgasm," she says. "No one ever does," Roscoe says. In London, Naomi Weis steps in front of a double decker bus.

In the middle of the night, Serum awakened Roscoe to tell him that Diego Maradona's henchman had arrived and did Roscoe want to meet them? Outside, three men in black suits smoked cigarettes next to the swimming pool. "Tell them I don't smoke," said Roscoe and slipped out the back second story window and zig-zagged through the back streets of Davis, heading for the Arco Punk Lounge. Once there, he ordered a shot and a beer and peered at the dance floor. To his relief, Naomi Weis was not there. Or maybe he was disappointed. He thought about his life. He was almost thirty. It was time to live differently. But a beautiful, almost brown young woman in skin tight jeans, wavy black hair and gold hoop earrings sidled up to him.

"Buy me a drink?" she said.

"Are you here alone?" he cautiously queried.

"For the time being."

"Single?"

"Venezuelan."

The band was covering "Mongoloid."

She threw back her shot of rum. "Let's dance," she said.

Well, it was just a dance. They jumped around. The song ended and she kissed him on the lips. Three muscular men in black t-shirts with Venezuela printed on their chests surrounded them.

"Oh-oh," she said.

Enter, of course, the Argentinians.

It would be years before Roscoe found out that Argentinians didn't even consider Venezuelans to be South American.

Roscoe tried to excuse himself. The Venezuelans blocked his exit. The Argentinians circled the Venezuelans.

At the edge of his mind, he heard someone whispering a poem. His life was about to change.

SNOW WHITE

THELMA AND LOUISE head east, don't they? Are they leaving men? I suppose I could Google the story, but though I prefer knowledge to ignorance (foregoing the pit of post-structural epistemology), I prefer imagination to knowledge (if Kant doomed Western metaphysics, he did wonders for Coleridge, who misinterpreted him), so Thelma and Louise are running, yes, running away, and so, aren't we all? Two women running away; it's 1991, but it feels like the eighties, two women, and isn't it about time? Louise is young, Thelma middle-aged. They pick up a sexy hitch hiker. Louise fucks him. They both fuck some men, they kill one in self defense, kind of by accident, of course. On the run from the law, then finally cornered by an army of over-armed police led by a rough, handsome sheriff who in his deep and conflicted inner toughness sympathetically yearns for their rugged, female independence, both empathically and sexually (man vs. woman, culture vs. nature, civilization vs. the Wild); they drive their convertible joyously over a cliff and the movie ends with them flying, forever and forever in flight, not in death but in flight. So now that's out of the way, or if in the way at least we're not pretending it's hidden.

Diosa and Kevorkian are about to head west. Diosa is twenty-six years old, Kevorkian forty-one. Diosa has cut her hair again, dyed it red, permed it into a curly mop; she wears big hoop earrings, ties a colorful scarf around her head. She's got $300 and a trunk full of shoes, some tops and jeans, a portable cassette player and headphones—she plugs into Bowie, "Modern Love." She wears too much make-up, as does Kevorkian, her hair a black explosion; she listens to *La Traviata*.

Neither of them has applied to the Ph.D. program at the University of Utah in Salt Lake City. Neither of them has ever been there. It's the dreamy West, redder than Mars, drier (dire?) and more golden than the moon; west of Kansas, west of Denver, south of Canada, a yawn from San Francisco in impossible California; in Salt Lake you can lie by a river in the valley, sunbathing, and watch it snow on the mountains beyond (that's what Twain said), planning your ski trip to Snowbird the next day; that's what Stephen M______, the King of Poetry said, he said don't bother to apply, he'd take care of it all. Could she bring Kevorkian? If it will bring you, he said. Do you know her work? I know everything, he said.

But before they took off, what did she do? Well, at first she ran away somewhere else. She met Ruth Sparrow who gave a workshop in Charlottesville and Sparrow invited her to flee to Vermont and take a vacation from the world of men. In Vermont, Ruth Sparrow taught her to tend a flower garden that lined the walk in front of her little house, to weed and water and prune the lilacs and lilies, the peonies and roses, hydrangeas, hibiscus, wisteria, tulips, daisies, daffodils, and gorgeous sunflowers raising their heads to the sun, and spices: rosemary, thyme, oregano, tarragon, parsley, basil, sage, catnip, and chives, all in their seasons, all in their balance, to watch and listen to the insects, the fertilizing bees, but most importantly to follow the birds, their perching, dance, song and flight, because everyone had a bird soul inside them, every woman at least, that must be freed and protected both, a task of depthful delicacy and, at times, grim determination. In the back of the house, of course, there was a vegetable garden that she and Ruth tended and harvested, cooked and canned for winter. They baked their own bread.

Ruth Sparrow and Diosa drank herb tea, lunched and dined, prepared food together and cleaned up together, because there was nothing like the music of women in a kitchen preparing and caring for each other. There were quiet times, alone, when each went off to write their poems, but for Diosa there was no creativity in bliss, and in those quiet moments she found her soul birdless, empty, her heart grasping for tense opposition, and she found herself filling her notebooks with the names ands smells of flowers, the songs and colors of birds, all to show Ruth, to please Ruth, the way she once wrote down the doggerel of the saints who spoke to her mother.

Then one day when Ruth was away, giving one of her many readings, Diosa looked up from a patch of blazing red gladiolas she was about to pick for the kitchen table and spotted a young woman watching her from behind a pine tree not far from the yard. Diosa went to her and the girl stepped out. She was small and dark, with wavy cropped hair, much like Ruth herself.

The girl put out her hand. "Has she named you after a bird yet?" she said. Diosa backed away. The air around them filled with voices, no, birdsong, though the twittering, the calls, seemed alarming.

"Girl poets," said the girl. "One night you fall asleep and you wake up in a cage, flapping, twittering." The young woman tilted her head and gazed at Diosa with one eye. She straightened. "The attic. Eventually she'll let you out. You'll be free, all right." She put out her hand again. "Raven," she said. "Her daughter."

Diosa took the hand and held it. Of course, under the circumstances, it felt a little like a claw.

"Runaways," Raven said. "Are you running away?"

"A nightingale who sits in the darkness and sings to soothe its own sweet sorrow," whispered Diosa.

"You wish," Raven said.

Diosa returned to the house and climbed to the attic where at the door she heard the tweeting and rattling of birds. The door was locked. Ruth Sparrow returned the next day with a new girl poet, Dianna Trix, a heroin addict, who Ruth brought home to cure and save.

"Ruined by a man, a pimp and addict," Ruth told Diosa. She locked Dianna Trix in the attic for a week. She came out looking flustered, but she wasn't addicted to heroin anymore, or poetry.

"Birds," she stuttered to Diosa.

"Did they recite any poetry?" Diosa said.

Trix tucked her nose under her arm. She'd cut her light brown hair into a fuzzy helmet with a slight ridge like a Mohawk down the middle. She lifted her head again. "I wasn't ruined by him," she said. "Unless you call ecstasy ruin."

"Ecstasy," said Diosa. She'd known a lot of men, but never ecstasy.

"You ran from ecstasy?"

"You can't possess ecstasy."

"Are you turning into a bird?"

Dianna Trix fluttered her elbows. "I have always been a bird," she said.

Ruth Sparrow came into the kitchen. She went to her cupboard and brought out two ceramic bowls. She gathered some almonds, yogurt, strawberries, went to the cutting board and began slicing the fruit. "Blue Jay," she said to Trix, "help me here." Her dark eyes met Diosa's. "Better this," she said, "than devastation."

Sparrow now doted on Blue Jay. She fed her and watched her as she ate, as she pecked at her nuts and fruit and seeds. Yet despite her apparent recovery it seemed, at best, that Blue Jay grew increasingly diminutive. And as Diosa went about her daily chores, it was almost as if she had disappeared from the household. When the three of them ate, Ruth and Blue Jay huddled together at the end of the table, sharing a plate, as Diosa prepared and served, cleared the setting as the two of them nuzzled and preened. One day, when Ruth took her station wagon to town to pick up supplies, Blue Jay disappeared. Diosa checked the garden, then the front yard. On the edge of the woods she heard only the soft ack-ack of a raven or crow. Back inside she found Blue Jay huddled, barefoot, at the top of the steps under the attic door. If now smaller than ever, her feet curled, and on her hands and face grew the intimation of soft down.

"I want to go in," whispered Blue Jay.

When Diosa got done helping Sparrow unload and stockpile the groceries, she confronted her. "She's at the attic door," she said to her.

"It's a process, my dear," said Ruth Sparrow. "She's finding her soul; not ready for captivity or freedom."

"And me?" Diosa asked.

"You don't realize how ruined you are," said Sparrow. "Take sanctuary. Relax into it."

Was that the choice? Diosa felt the base of her nose hardening into her cheeks. That afternoon, yearning for ruin, she went back to the woods, looking for Raven, but the air around her was filled with a cloud of flapping birds, with whistles, chatter, and twitter. She called for the girl, hoping for her to emerge, a single raven or crow, but there were dozens of them, not silent but screaming. She listened for voices beneath the cries, but there was nothing in them but the fears and desires of birds.

Of course her car wouldn't start. She walked to the road and hitched a ride to town from a duck hunter in a pick-up truck, middle aged, red checked jacket, billed cap. "Bird girl?" he said.

"You shoot them?" she said. "Love them?"

"Just ducks. Doves sometimes. Wild pigeons."

"Around here?"

"They have to be in flight. Can't shoot'em in the water or out of a tree. Can you fly?"

She held out her arms.

"You look a little like a bird," he said.

"You look a little like a bird," said Diosa.

"Big Bird," said the duck hunter, and laughed.

"So shoot me."

"You ain't flying," the duck hunter said. He laughed again.

"Stop the truck," said Diosa. And he did. She opened the door and stepped out, raised her arms. Went up on her toes.

"You ain't flying," said the duck hunter.

Diosa began to bounce on her toes, delicate, ballet-like, soft, graceful, it almost seemed as if she gained more air with each bounce. A breeze swept through the pines like a song. *A man once loved a woman so much,* sang Diosa to the tuneful wind, *that he killed her, so he could know for sure no other man could have her.*

"Let me get my gun in case you take off," said the duck hunter.

But by the time he got in and out of the truck she was long gone.

At the auto repair shop, Raven crawled out from underneath an old Buick. She wore black pants, a black t-shirt, black sneakers, black longshoreman's cap, tattoo of a raven on her left bicep. "You got past the duck guy," she said.

"Flew," said Diosa. "Away."

"Nobody gets out unscathed," said Raven. "Want me to go fix your car?"

"Flight is exhausting," Diosa said.

"For now," said Raven. "But orgasm will never be the same."

They got in the tow truck. Nice big truck. Diosa put her feet on the dash.

"You got nice feet," Raven said.

"I still got feet," said Diosa.

"And a new beak," said Raven.

Diosa checked the rear view mirror. Her nose seemed a little more hawk-like. "There's always plastic surgery," she said.

"You look more beautiful than ever," said Raven. "I majored in engineering."

"Engineering is poetry."

"I'm a mechanic."

"Mechanism is poetry," said Diosa.

"My older sister was a poet," said Raven. "She ran away to Santa

Catalina and became a flying fish."

"She'll land in my boat one day," said Diosa.

"Maybe she will," Raven said.

"Or be eaten by a shark."

"We've all already been eaten by sharks," Raven said. She reached the turn-off for her mother's cottage and drove through a junkyard of small cars, a flock of junk. Nothing more need be said, really. "Do you think there's more than this?"

"Do you mean after this?" said Diosa.

"I mean everywhere."

They reached Diosa's white 2002. They got out of the truck. Raven opened the BMW's hood, reattached the distributor cap. "The hills are alive," said Raven. She kissed Diosa on the lips. It was a soft, experienced kiss. "Nice," said Raven. "Want to make love?"

"We already have," whispered Diosa. "A thousand times."

"This time," said Raven.

Diosa started her car. She stepped out and kissed Raven again.

"This time," said Diosa, "I'm saving your life."

"This time," said Raven, "I'm saving *your* life."

And so they did, there, in the woods, but not like birds, nor spirits, but bodies, in the way we save and destroy our lives each time we make love, falling deeper into our souls and closer to nothing; something a woman can do and survive and a man cannot, even if he thinks he does. They lay with each other till morning, dressed, and parted. Raven stepped back. When she raised her arms, black feathers fell. "Well caw-caw to that," said Raven. "I'll come back later for my truck." She hopped twice, spread her wings, and took off, a black bird in the blue sky. Though in minutes it seemed the sky was full of stars, then clouds, and then the sky fell in sheets of rain.

There were thousands of Elvis impersonators, but this one really looked like Elvis, and not the old, fat one either who, in her poetic heart, Diosa really preferred, but the young one, thighs hard, shirt sleeves rolled up at his dancing biceps, belly muscles vibrating. This was Graceland before Disney got hold of it (before Morgan-Stanley could bring meaning to your money)—not that Disney doesn't have its own ghosts—no Lisa Pressley headsets, no sixteen gift shops, each placed before and after a Graceland divided into eight separate exhibits; Graceland is here yet a mansion filled by Elvis, and one girl guide walks you through and talks: the gold and black leather paneled three TV basement—he could watch all three networks at once—the jungle room with its twisted wooden throne; you couldn't go upstairs where he died on the toilet (just like Jack Kerouac) (and you still can't); the memorabilia room had his picture where he's totally fucked up getting his anti-drug sheriff badge from Nixon (now it's gone), there was a porno film theater (now it's his karate workout gym); you didn't have to pay extra to see his cars or get in his private jet (gift shops now on either side of both); there were horses, some that he owned, still alive in the pasture beyond. Diosa and Kevorkian were on the last tour of the day. The setting sun reddened. The group had moved on while Diosa lingered at Elvis' grave, and it was the same, as when in Teotihuacán she stood impossibly atop El Templo de la Luna, her arms, her wrinkled hands, reached out to La Avenida del Muerte to the giant Templo del Sol; the setting sun emblazoned a red ruby on her finger; Roscoe bought it for her at the Anapurna Hotel in Kathmandu the night the Maoists bombed it and the hotel fell around them in ashes and he stripped her there in the hot gray snow and they made love like fallen angels in the ashes; now he's dead and a hummingbird has flown to the base of Quetzalcoatl's temple and alighted on the stone serpent's head; the feathered serpent, a blue shadow, crawled up the steps, flew to El Templo del Sol, perched atop and turned; even he would have her and die, his skeletal tongue a bone licking her pelvis, the last thing of him to die; here she decides once again on her nothingness, deep nothingness, not nothingness holier than thou; deeper; Quetzalcoatl inhales and stops the sun, the earth ceases to roll and the hummingbird, Huitzilopochtli, sword laden, flies to her fingertips; she thinks, end, end, but it does not end.

The fringe on Elvis' jacket, thrown over his shoulder, falls like down, then flutters in the wind. I met your friend there in 1957, he says. She knows the story. Kevorkian met him then, in San Antonio, when she was Miss Texas.

"Hubba hubba," Diosa said.

"Love me tender," said Elvis. "Here on my grave."

Okay, fuck it, he was already dead. And it wouldn't be the first time she'd done it on a grave or with a ghost. Ghosts were neither mortal nor immortal. Ghosts crossed time like bottles on the sea. They fell into families, into tribes, into loneliness. There could be as many Elvis ghosts as there were Elvis impersonators, and not the ghosts of impersonators, but ghosts who were impersonators, for who would come back as a ghost of herself?

"*Perhaps,*" said Diosa, "*we're trapped innately, gnat-like, in the middle of great vacant signs.*"

"Maybe we ourselves are the vacant signs," Elvis said. "Thank you very much."

If that wasn't enough to convince her that this wasn't Elvis.

Back in the car, searching for a campground, Kevorkian said, "I fucked him in '57. I was young. Impressionable."

Diosa put on her headphones to listen to "Modern Love." "Was he poetical?" she said.

"In a lithe, visceral sort of way," said Kevorkian. She yawned.

They camped at Horr Lake, south of town. They had to pay for their campsite. They had to buy wood for their fire and then a license to burn it. Kevorkian gave the ranger another five.

"Where's the license," she said.

"I'll remember you," the ranger said.

"I'll remember you," said Kevorkian.

"I hope you do," said the ranger.

Later, by the fire, they ate tinned smoked oysters and drank red wine.

Diosa kept the wine bottle in a brown bag. "Think this is a dry county?"

"We didn't buy a drinking license," said Kevorkian. "Why do I find all this so suspicious?"

"He's going to show up here," said Diosa.

"Oh God," said Kevorkian. "Have you ever got laid really good? I wouldn't mind him showing up if I knew he could do it."

"You can't tell by looking?"

"No."

"Well not him," said Diosa.

That's when he showed up. He stopped his truck in front of their fire and got out. He was young, African-American, but this being Memphis, everybody in the campground was African-American. "Need help with that fire?" the ranger asked.

The two women looked at their blazing little fire and then looked back at him.

"Will it cost another five dollars?" Kevorkian said.

He pointed toward their tent. "You got a skunk in your groceries," he said.

Sure enough, a black and white tail twitched at the top of their grocery bag wherein lay their hot dogs, buns, coffee and donuts.

"The old skunk in the bag routine," said Kevorkian.

Diosa said, "Does this trick work in bars?"

"Do you want me to get that skunk out of your bag or not?" said the ranger.

That was a good question because it was hard to know what was being negotiated. The ranger stepped toward the bag, grabbed the skunk tail and flung the skunk into the air, skunk stink following like a putrid rainbow. The skunk hit the ground stinking and running.

"It still stinks," said Kevorkian.

"Not as much as it would have," said the ranger. He got back in his truck. "White chicks," he said and drove off.

The next day they ate spaghetti in St. Louis. In Topeka every bar was a strip club, which is what Bill Burroughs told them in a café in Lawrence where they found him asleep at a corner table. "A hornets' nest of pornography lunch fests," drawled Burroughs. "Businests. Businessmen gone wild. Unfortunately it's very conventional stuff."

"I was Pheda Lamort's roommate," Diosa told him. Pheda had sent him a book of porno poems that Burroughs loved.

"That girl had talent. What happened to her?"

"She became a mountain."

"I'm familiar with that fate," said Burroughs. "It can happen when your back is turned."

So for lunch they watched strippers in Topeka, girls dancing naked on the bar.

"Poor things," said Kevorkian.

"All that love," said Diosa. "This is why I'm not a Christian."

They turned down dozens of free drinks, made it to west Kansas amidst spreading golden fields of sunflowers.

"Well there, Oz makes sense," Kevorkian said. Looking for a motel, they stopped in Goodland, a town that had nothing in it, a dead traffic light swinging in the wind at the center of town. A cow stood in the street. Tall, silver grain silos towered around them, rusted train cars and train tracks. It was one of the new dead cities of the west. There are, in fact, many.

"An island of nothing floating on nothing," said Kevorkian.

"Just like life itself," said Diosa, thinking presciently or remembering the future, that feeling, knowing you knew something you weren't ready to know.

"Milk a cow?" said Kevorkian.

"Rob a bank?" Diosa said.

Well they'd need to find a bank. They strolled down the vacant middle of the ghost streets.

"Is emptiness the gift of the dead," said Diosa. "Brown owls in a blue evening. Blue pollens. Brown trees."

Two poets in a ghost town. What better? What worse?

"Do you ever think about Neal Cassady?" Kevorkian said to the wind.

"Je pense a Dean Moriarty," said Diosa. "No."

"He was born in Salt Lake City," said Kevorkian. "Mormon Central. A tremendous irony, don't you think?"

"Not half as much now as when we get there. He died on railroad tracks like Anna Karenina."

"In Mexico," said Kevorkian.

"A brakeman. A lover."

"A fucker."

"Fucked everybody," said Diosa.

"Everything unfolds," said Kevorkian.

"Everything unfolds and folds and unfolds."

"Why am I feeling we shouldn't go to Salt Lake?" said Kevorkian.

"Don't have your second thoughts first," said Diosa, rather uncharacteristically, but Kevorkian could bring that out in you. "First your first thoughts, then your second thoughts. That's logic. Look, there's a bank."

A little brick building, a sign atop saying Bank of Goodland, and sure enough a man inside, a young man, though short and thick, a reddish-blond buzz-cut, black glasses, he stood in front of the bank counter, staring left as if waiting for a bus or a train. The women walked in, Diosa holding the door. "Holy smokes," the young man said, "it's my lucky day."

"It's your unlucky day," said Diosa.

"Give us your cash," Kevorkian said.

The young banker pulled out his wallet and emptied it onto the floor. A tangle of bills fell like moths, flittering, landing, fading away.

"Bank money?" Kevorkian said.

"We only got ghost dollars here," said the young banker. "Let me buy you girls a beer."

"Ghost beer?" Diosa said.

The banker put his wallet back in his pocket and headed out the door. They followed. The sign atop the bank now said Ghostland.

"That said Goodland," said Kevorkian.

"Only to the uninitiated," said the young banker. "I never understood the lyrics to 'Hotel California' either, but then I'm not a ghost."

"Songwriters thinking ahead to their ghostliness," Diosa said.

"Maybe I'm a ghost after all," he said, "though really, how would I know? Do you think ghosts are like misty wisps in space?"

"The ones I've seen," said Kevorkian.

"Those aren't ghosts. Those are visages," the young banker said. He rubbed his buzz cut with his hands as they followed him down the naked street. A train whistled, then they could hear its black rumble. "That's it," said the banker. "The train of the past. Quite visceral in its way, not a wisp."

On the nearby train tracks, beneath the silos, the tracks hissed and the air rumbled, the click-click-click of the passing cars.

"Empty, of course," said the banker.

"Or full of ghosts?" said Kevorkian. "Does it stop at graveyards?"

"Undoubtedly. But don't go Cartesian or Tibetan with it," said the banker, rubbing his head again. "I've done it. You just end up where you started. The question is: why is all this in front of your face?"

"Why what?" said Diosa.

"That's the answer."

"What's the question?"

"Right," said the banker, "Gertrude Stein. It's the not there there and it ends there. Let's get those beers."

They came to an old, crumbling warehouse with corrugated metal walls and entered through a tiny door. Inside, a beer hall full of men, not businessmen like in Topeka, men in jeans and shirts and overalls, no naked dancing women; no women at all. All of them turned at once and said in unison, "Girls!" A juke box came alive playing "Hotel California."

The young, stocky banker rubbed his head and looked at Diosa. "I'm not making this up, you are," he said. "Are you a surrealist?"

"Not yet," she said.

"That train is someone else's memory," he said. "Not yours."

Whose?" said Diosa.

They sat. The banker went to the bar and came back with three bottles of Budweiser.

"A couple came by here on motorcycles. The girl was really young. They spent the night in a sunflower field. Someone drove through the field in his pick-up and killed the girl.

"Messy?" said Kevorkian.

"Kansas," said the banker. "I'm not from here. Minnesota." He told them he'd moved there with his wife who got a job in a federal prison some seventy miles north. Ghostland was cheap. There were empty houses, sort of, you could just move into but for the ghostly recriminations. He waved toward the bar. "They shoot anything that moves. I think they all shot each other."

"But not you," said Kevorkian.

"How would I know anymore."

"Your wife?"

"Hasn't been home for a while."

"I can imagine," Kevorkian said.

"Imagine away." He double rubbed his head again. "Started hearing the train after the biker, the guy who lived, took off. Said the girl died everywhere they went. The girl follows him. The train follows him."

"Stay away from the tracks," said Diosa. "That's my philosophy of life."

"You have a philosophy of life?" said Kevorkian.

Every man in the room turned toward them and shouted in unison,

"The train!"

"You wouldn't want to take me with you," said the young banker. "You can understand."

"We're stuffed to the gills," Kevorkian said.

"I can make myself very tiny," said the desperate young banker. He pulled out a blues harp. "And entertaining."

It's inevitable that if you're to have two women driving cross-country then at some point there'll be a man involved, the problem being that the banker, whose name was Glen—however convoluted and obscure, even potentially ghostly, he might be—was unassuming in every way, about as sexy as a sunflower seed. Maybe he was violent. We'll see. But he was a good packer, having once worked in a warehouse when on a trip to New York City he was fleeced of everything he owned by a wizened and infamous prostitute who convinced him in an hour that she was a wealthy widow and that she loved him and would give him everything she owned rather than die without his love. She couldn't bring him right home to her house in New Rochelle because her ailing mother was staying with her there, but she took him to a hotel somewhere on Houston. Got him drunk, drugged him, and left him with nothing but his boxers. He didn't even get laid. On the street like that, in lower Manhattan, he fit right in, but for being recognized by Roscoe's younger brother, Roland, who not so many years previous had the same thing happen to him. Now Roland managed a furniture warehouse in Long Island City manned by a dozen other past victims of the White Widow, Roland having taken it upon himself to hire anybody he found down to their underpants on the streets of lower Manhattan. You can imagine the stories in that warehouse; it was like the *Decameron*. Anyway, that's where Glen, the young banker, learned to pack so good. He rearranged the trunk and back seat of Diosa's 1969 BMW 2002 until there was a tiny space behind the driver and slipped right in. They headed west, the shadows of ghost trains rumbling behind them, yet as Diosa drove through the flat and rolling plains of sunflowered west Kansas, she thought of the dead girl, the motorcycle rider who died under the wheels of a pick-up truck—where were the female ghosts of Ghostland?—behind her, Glen the banker said, "At the hair salon, but you can't get a beer at the hair salon," though she bet you *could* get a beer there, and a shot of tequila, too; she wondered if they shouted like a Greek chorus like the men or hissed in whispers in some language of women.

"We should go back," she said.

"Let's just get to Denver," said Kevorkian.

"Would the girl be there?" said Diosa. "The motorcyclist?"

"No," said Glen. "She's not that kind of ghost."

"The train," she said.

"You're babbling," said Kevorkian.

Diosa thought of the fine line between the inevitable and the impossible; she felt the road beneath her weaving back and forth across that line. She remembered a future dream she would have in Salt Lake City. She awoke in a one bedroom apartment, a bathroom and a hot plate; she lived with three cats who sent her their dreams: a female tabby dreamed she was a wild horse; a male tuxedo cat dreamed of trains in the night, trains that stopped at graveyards like train stations, ghosts boarding and departing; a giant orange cat dreamed that it snowed and snowed, the night quieted, the air filled with silent white, and in the morning when it stopped a knock came on Diosa's door and when she opened it, a man stood there, blond and blue eyed, the shadow of a beard—he was not the greatest living poet in America—and she took him in her arms and brought him inside and there, on the floor, made love to him.

"Let's go to Vegas," Glen said.

"A bit out of the way," Kevorkian said.

"We'll lose a day," said Glen. "What's a day?"

But a time would come, certainly it would come, when a day would mean everything; she thought of time, men's time with its moments ticking inexorably forward, consecutive, abrupt, causal; and women's time, like Woolf's, years collapsing into seconds, seconds expanding into decades, a birth, a life, a death in a blink; she sees herself in thirty years, sitting across from her lover; they had a daughter who grew up and moved away to an invisible city; their own lives now parenthetical, she turns to him; I will grow old and die alone, she says and he says, I live as if I never happened at all; lives disappearing inside lives, the world crowded with unreachable memories, invisible memories, not dreams, memories of dreams, not Einstein, not time stretching on the back of space with its spontaneous certainty; Vishnu awakens and the cosmos disappears, reappears in his milky millennial blink, shivers, shimmers under his half-closed, half-open lids; she hung a left, bending the car south.

Without any irony Vegas dutifully disregarded time and even temperature. There was no sky. They got a room in the Oriental Palace for $18, just in case. Glen pulled out his harmonica. "I'm going to busk for a few bucks, then make a million," he said. Kevorkian, already disenchanted, planned to window shop, kitty-corner, at Caesars Palace. Diosa, colored scarf wrapped around her head, red hair flowing out, walked the strip, felt a slot machine inside the Flamingo and danced in, not danced, it just looked like a dance to the manager who over-saw the help who scanned the gambling floor with cameras in the ceiling above; now, of course, inevitably, here in a casino, his chance desire an allegory of destiny. Diosa knew she'd be good at slots. How can you be good at slots? The surveillance manager, his heart like a swan, sent an arrow down as she approached a machine, fruits and bars, and felt an intimacy there, they both did, as she put a quarter in the machine and pulled the handle (that's how it was done then); three cherries; eight quarters clanged down. Three more quarters, three bars; the machine rioted and she had a hundred bucks. Diosa filled two big plastic cups and sat. The manager was at her side.

He was handsome in his way, at forty. A dark, full head of hair falling slightly over his ears, brown eyes that reflected the despair sagging all around him, the aisles of people repetitiously pouring money into the machines; you could hear the cheery blinging and donging of falling coins everywhere, but you couldn't see it anywhere. He had a Flamingo badge shaped like a flamingo on his suit jacket that said Ron Cotto.

"Even when they win," he said to Diosa, "they've already lost more than they could ever win back, and so they'll lose that too. Not an old, tired metaphor. Reality."

It wasn't as if she knew of all the deaths that followed her love, not yet, besides, love follows death and death follows love, this was enough to know. She met his stare. He fell into her eyes, even in this light bluer than a star. He'd left a wife and child in New Jersey. Failed as a stand-up comic in New York. Took a job as a personnel manager at the Big Apple Circus. He jumped the circus while it was wintering in South Carolina where he met a blonde motel lounge singer named Bonnie, fell into sex, not love, and traveled with her here because she wanted to perform in Vegas, but she didn't make it; not at all; she left him for a gold mine foreman from Rock Springs, Wyoming. Just as well, so he came to Vegas himself. He could play the bass and got a job with a Bruce Springsteen impersonator, and even if the band was pretty good, it was too early for that to catch on, though he did get laid a lot. Now this. He told her this as he walked with her to the bar.

He was, in his way, a charismatic. He emitted charisma, and it got him this far, a god of gambling, one of many, but one of them, and now, at forty, looking back and looking ahead, urged by desperation, at the edge or end of his banal success, insipidly and momentously unfulfilled.

Diosa, her hand now on his arm, stood on a cusp as well, but a woman lived on cusps, loved on them, something a man would never understand. And she knew what it meant to accept a drink. But what would it mean to accept a man, an ordinary man, this man, for a night, a night of affection, warmth, with luck some adoration, an orgasm, mythical whispers of love and plans, as real as anything else that had ever happened and now was gone, as real as anything that might happen but did not.

He cashed her quarters. As they reached the bar, her arm on his, his life was exploding like an asterisk. He wanted to ask her if she believed in love at first sight, but she was too savvy, he could see that; she ordered a gin martini, dry, twist, a drink she'd learned from Swift, a real drink, not a girly drink; his brow bent and she saw it. He drank scotch, neat.

"I'm wise for my years," she said to him.

"I'm falling in love," he said, but his tone was ambiguous enough; he might have said it a thousand times before, though even if he had, even if he'd said it a thousand times, half meaning it and half not, this time he meant it.

She said, "I'm leaving tomorrow."

"Maybe you won't," he said. "Maybe you'll stay here. Maybe we'll run away."

She liked that. And seeing she could never love him opened the possibility for love, if only for a night. She thought now of how many men she had ever really loved, though now, looking back, it was impossible to tell; how did you gauge? by duration? intensity? She'd been married to Swift. Hadn't she loved him at times? And Hoppie, her first. Was it her love that killed them or her consent? Weren't we dead the moment we fell in love?

"I could make you rich," Ron Cotto said.

"Without risking your job?"

"I'd risk anything."

"Your career?"

"Career is a dirty word," he said.

She worried that he wasn't rough enough around the edges. He believed, in that moment, that he really would do anything for her. She saw him falling into her, cocooning into her complexities; he might emerge depressed, ruined, or transformed; he might not emerge. That again.

"Midnight at Caesars. Cleopatra's Barge," he said. He kissed her forehead. Her lips.

She had to admit, it felt good.

She found Kevorkian in the Forum, staring at a window of shoes.

"I'm already too old to wear most of them," Kevorkian said. "But not you. You have great legs."

"Let's get out of here before I kill somebody," said Diosa.

In the room Glen was counting out a stack of bills. His busking was a disaster. He couldn't really play the harmonica that well. But poking from the inside of his pocket it looked like a gun. "You just have to pick a winner," he said. "No sense holding up a sad person."

"It's hard to believe," said Kevorkian.

"Everything is hard to believe," said Diosa.

Glen gathered his cash. "This is not ghost money!" he said.

"Why didn't we pick up a handsome, romantic young drifter?" Kevorkian said.

"With a big dick?" said Glen.

"Maybe," said Kevorkian.

"I have money now," said Glen. "That's almost as good."

"Almost," said Diosa.

They crossed the northwest corner of Arizona along the Virgin River Canyon, into Virgin, Utah where a thousand Mormons died of starvation when Brigham Young divided his territory into quadrants and sent his colonists into the barren wilds without even knowing what was where. Now there were only a few abandoned shacks. Talk about red cliffs and ghosts.

St. George was mobbed with women and girls in bonnets and pioneer dresses.

"This bodes ill," Kevorkian said.

"Time for me to fess up," said Glen. "I'm an outcast from a polygamist colony."

And what was that. It took Glen a while to explain it. Now you can just go watch back episodes of *Big Love*.

"I wasn't planning it, but now that I'm back I think I'm going to kill my uncles and fathers," said Glen.

"Fathers?"

"It's hard to keep it all straight," he said. "That's how I got thrown out."

"Not straight enough," said Diosa.

"And liberate the women?" said Kevorkian.

"And take over!" said Glen, rubbing his head. "Why liberate them? They're pre-oppressed."

"So we picked up a murderer after all," said Kevorkian.

"He's not sexy," said Diosa.

"Not yet!" said Glen.

And that was that for Glen, a red herring of life.

Diosa and Kevorkian headed north, Cedar City, Richfield, Nephi, Heber City. Following the river, the gorge; not yet fall, the sun poured on the pine forests that spread on the mountains.

A car passed them with a bumper sticker: "Yup, urine Utah."

"Salt Lake City," said Kevorkian.

"Here we come," said Diosa.

"And what about the wife?" Kevorkian finally said.

"I don't want to be his wife."

"Just his queen."

"Of poetry," Diosa said.

"Maybe this was all a little rash," said Kevorkian.

"A big rash," said Diosa.

"A 2,500 mile rash," said Kevorkian.

They mowed into Salt Lake. They found Kevorkian's rented house, across the street from a huge cemetery. Diosa had a room attached to the back, but she didn't go in just yet. She walked across the street and scaled the graveyard wall, stared across the dead quiet, the obelisks of Mormon elders surrounded by the tiny markers of women that said only "Mother," and the smaller-still graves of dozens of children. Mother. Was that enough to live by? To die? Did the ghost train stop here? She felt a blue aura rise from her forehead. A song, Annette Funicello, singing "How Will I Know My Love?" She felt like Snow

White waking up from the dead. She went back to the house.

"I'll never write a poem for anyone I love," she said to Kevorkian.

"Or loved?"

"I'm going now," Diosa said.

"Maybe I'll just move to San Francisco," Kevorkian said.

"Next stop, the future," said Diosa. Anyway, who knew? Twenty-six years old, she thought she might know. She found Stephen M______'s home in the Avenues. Straightened her scarf. Checked her eye shadow. Walked to his door.

HIS WINGS

THAT NIGHT IN THE BAR Roscoe broke a bottle over the head of a Venezuelan. He went to jail because the guy almost died. At least Carona Petras couldn't follow him there (she married a history professor from Cal Poly, inherited and sold the moving company, became an arts mogul on the Central Coast).

In jail, Roscoe got placed on a chain gang that maintained county parks. He was the only guy on the gang who wasn't Mexican, including the supervisors. Besides learning a lot of Spanish, he learned, as he'd learned on the garbage truck, that it was easier to work hard than avoid work. But jail was bad for his love life.

Yet these were days of simplicity. Soon he got promoted to work with county crews. He could even sleep at Buzz's. They'd taken his driver's license, but he could wake up at dawn and bicycle to the jail, check in and head out with the crew, riding on the bumper of the dump truck, just like in his garbage days; they got dumped off at a park with an assignment for the day; after work he got dropped off at the jail at five to check out. He mowed lawns, weeded flower beds, took a hose into the lavs and blasted them clean, walls, sinks, toilets; it got so incongruously wet in there. But he was good at it, trustworthy, hardworking; the crews fought over who would get him on their truck. Often they just left him alone at a park and went off to get drunk, picking him up at five. Finally a judge gave him a park of his own. His own park; he called it Roscoe Park. The only hard part was he didn't get paid. At dawn he bicycled to the jail, signed in, then biked to his park, spent the day mowing and weeding, collecting trash, hosing down the bathrooms. And though a big apartment complex sat across the street, with plenty of activity in front of it, mostly prostitution and drug deals, no one ever used the park. Roscoe could finish his day before lunch if he wanted and spend the afternoon under the picnic shelter reading Goethe or counting his breaths. Then he signed out at the jail and courthouse and rode home.

But one day, when he arrived in the morning, a man in one-piece overalls—though gray, not like the one-piece orange ones that prisoners wore—stood near the picnic shelter. He was big, a little taller and broader than Roscoe, thick footed, a broad forehead and chin, skin almost brown, almost blue, with eyes indiscernibly gray, eyes that glowed with intense and vacuous innocence. He plodded toward Roscoe.

"I'm working with you now," he said to Roscoe.

"I don't need help," Roscoe said.

"I do," said the man. His voice was thick and gentle. "I might not seem to be all here because a lot of me is someplace else."

Roscoe turned from him and walked toward the trash pokers that leaned against the lavs. He didn't want to know where that place might be.

"It's indescribable," the man said.

Roscoe handed him a trash poker. "Indescribable," he said.

"I learned that word from God," said the man.

"Any others?" said Roscoe.

"Some others."

"You'll let me know which ones."

The man smiled at him, his eyes narrowing, his forehead slouching. Roscoe couldn't really tell if he was young or old. His face was quiet and smooth. His hair was thick and fuzzy, yet sprinkled with silver-gray. Roscoe handed him a plastic trash bag.

"You're supposed to take care of me," the man said.

"I'm taking care of you," said Roscoe.

"I might appear slow," he said.

"You're fine," said Roscoe. "We don't need speed."

The man grinned. Their eyes met. There were other universes in those eyes.

"It's a good thing people litter or we wouldn't get to do this," said the man.

Roscoe spread his arms. "They must do it at night," he said.

"Oh, they must!" said the man.

Roscoe introduced himself. The man said his name was Gabe. He was really good at stretching the mouths of trash bags around the cement trash containers in a single motion. He had, as he said, a technique.

Now, in the mornings, when Roscoe arrived, Gabe was waiting. Same simple look. Same overalls. Their job now, after trash and bathrooms, was to dig up the grass from under the trees, then dig a trench around the trees for watering. The big trees were particularly hard.

"And they don't need it," said Gabe.

"No?"

"They have developed root systems that stretch way out."

Roscoe leaned on his shovel. On top of working all day he was bicycling everywhere. He was getting in shape.

"How long have you been helping like this, Gabe?" he said.

"You're helping me," said Gabe.

"Where do you go?"

"Go?"

"After work."

"Let's eat lunch," said Gabe.

Gabe always brought and ate the same thing. Under a tree he opened his brown paper bag and ate a sort of wafer, that with what looked like a slice of white cheese, and something milk-like; it was hard to tell. Roscoe just drank water from his canteen. He didn't eat lunch.

"People think I'm limited," Gabe said.

"Slow?" said Roscoe.

"Slow like a plant," Gabe said. He offered Roscoe a bit of wafer. "Try this."

Roscoe did. It was flat, almost tasteless. But once he ate it, something changed. Things that were moving, people, cars, bicycles, began to race so fast that they disappeared. Beneath him, he felt the tree roots stretching, above him he heard the breaths of leaves and in the branches he understood the singing birds, though he couldn't translate the language, he simply understood.

"Not limited," Gabe said to him. "Limitless."

When the wafer wore off Roscoe stood. Time had passed, hours, and they were supposed to have moved a dozen railroad ties to reinforce a hill behind the bathrooms. There was a long, two-handled cart that they were to load two ties at a time and roll them to the hill.

"I've never taken a drug like that before," Roscoe said.

"It's not a drug," said Gabe.

"We lost the afternoon."

"Don't worry," Gabe said. He walked, slowly, of course, to the pile of ties that the supervisor dropped off that morning. He picked up one railroad tie, tucked it under his arm, then another, and impossibly a third, and walked them to the hill. Roscoe could barely lift the end of one.

When Gabe came back Roscoe said, "Let's use the cart."

"We don't need the cart," said Gabe. "Wait at the hill. You can help me there."

At the bottom of the hill, after he delivered the rest of the ties, Gabe began to lay the railroad ties, half to half, like bricks. Roscoe hammered them together with rebar rods, using a sledge. He could barely keep up. When they came to the end of a row, needing only a half tie to complete it, Gabe snapped the tie in half over his knee. In no time they'd reinforced the hill.

Roscoe, whose clothes hung on him with sweat, stood with Gabe whose body glistened, almost silver, eminent with a kind of, well, effortless virtue.

"Your heart never closed to me," Gabe said to him. "Now you've seen the smallest slice of heaven."

"I'll let you drive the lawn mower tomorrow," Roscoe said.

It was as if Gabe's laughter fell from the sky.

Weeks passed. Roscoe was reaching the end of his jail time. He wondered if he should try to get in touch with Dandy, go back to school, bide time. He wasn't too old yet to do something, something besides read books, get fucked up, work. Every morning he awoke at dawn and bicycled to the jail, signed in, and then bicycled to the park where Gabe stood waiting under the picnic shelter. Everyday they worked in the quiet of the valley sun as if the park were separated from everything. No one seemed to use it, not the drug dealers, nor prostitutes, nor the women with baby carriages, nor kids on tricycles across the way outside the apartment complex.

"No one uses this park," Roscoe said to Gabe.

"That's why it's here," said Gabe.

But by now Roscoe was beyond thinking that anything, particularly his conversations with Gabe, would make any sense. During lunch, Gabe brought out his milk bottle, touched the liquid inside with his finger and then touched Roscoe's forehead. In a split second, for a split second, the world spread from him in quiet, understandable infinity, like the rays of substance in Spinoza.

"You live like this?" he said to Gabe.

"Everything does," Gabe said.

Then they worked together, silently, and then Roscoe bicycled to sign out at the jailhouse, went home to Buzz's, ate a peanut butter sandwich and drank a beer, then slept blissfully till dawn, dreamless but for some deep awareness, as if sleeping under the shadow of God, or under Vishnu's eyelid, the world only a dream away yet never dreamed.

He was in his last week of jail time, at the end of the workday, when the earthquake hit. He'd been hosing the men's room when the building shook radically, the cement walls groaning and cracking. Worse than anything was the grinding roar and rumble, as if a thousand trains were passing through. He fell to his knees and crawled out of the lav. In the twenty seconds of a big quake lies an hour of fear. And when it stops, the air still trembles, as if the world was filled with the memory, yet the quiet is quieter than silence.

Roscoe found Gabe outside the picnic shelter. There were yet no sirens. The city was on its back, knocked out. Across the way, the federal housing apartment complex had collapsed, and now came the first moans of the victims inside.

Gabe opened his lunch bag and offered Roscoe a small piece of the cheese stuff that he often ate with his wafer. Roscoe ate it. He felt the inside of his body explode and the outside expand to accommodate it. He felt gigantic. They crossed the street to the complex where a few people now staggered into the street. Where the second story had collapsed on the first, Gabe found a corner and lifted it onto his shoulder like Atlas, then Roscoe went inside and dragged women, children, and injured men into the street. Though it seemed to Roscoe to take place in a matter of seconds, he and Gabe worked long into the night, Gabe lifting cement foundations, Roscoe picking up the wounded in his arms, carrying them into the park and laying them down under the picnic shelter. The first aftershock hit. The complex shifted and settled, but by then they had most of the people out.

Gabe pulled out his container of milky liquid. This time he told Roscoe to sip it and then told him to place his hand on any injury: a cut, a broken limb, a cracked skull, a pulse-less heart; wounds closed, bones mended, bruises vanished, hearts beat again. The dazed occupants slowly arose, left the park, and joined their neighbors who stood by their cars and vans, trying to listen to dead radios.

Near dawn came the first sirens; police, paramedics and fire personnel finally arrived, sifting through the rubble, questioning the apartment dwellers.

"They won't remember anything," Gabe said to Roscoe. "Do you want to remember?"

"Yes," said Roscoe.

"Gabe touched Roscoe's forehead. "It won't matter," he said.

"A dream," Roscoe said.

"The line between memory and dream."

So there was nothing to put together, nothing to explain. The line between quark and galaxy, breath and miracle, life and death.

Now Gabe placed his right palm on Roscoe's heart. For a moment, he remembered the dream of the girl in the lake, her palm on his chest. It made Gabe smile a little. Roscoe wanted to say something, something like, This park doesn't really exist, but he knew that to be both true and absurd.

Gabe put his hands together in front of his chest. Enormous gray wings appeared on his back.

"These aren't mine," Gabe said to him. "I borrowed them." When Roscoe didn't answer, Gabe said, "From you." And then he disappeared.

Roscoe went to the picnic shelter and fell asleep. He stayed there for days and days, sleeping, waking, drinking a little water. He sat, legs folded, contemplating the ruins of the crumbled apartment complex where every day nothing happened. He didn't know how many days and nights went by, but one day he decided to go home.

Buzz met him at the door.

"There's a bench warrant here for your arrest," said Buzz. "For breaking jail."

"How long?" said Roscoe.

"Forty days," said Buzz. "The police came here. I saved this." He showed Roscoe a photo on the front page of the *Davis Enterprise* of a crumbled apartment complex. "Nobody died. Nobody was even hurt. Nobody remembers anything."

Roscoe said nothing.

"That's across form your park?" said Buzz.

Roscoe read the bench warrant. "I was already in jail," he said. "They could have found me in the park."

"They went to the park," Buzz said.

Roscoe went to his room. He gathered up some t-shirts and sweat shirts, another pair of jeans, his sleeping bag, a jacket. He put on his riding boots. He said good-bye to Buzz, jumped on his motorcycle and headed for Vancouver. Much of the rest you already know.

ASK WHAT YOU LIKE

A MAN STOOD on the sidewalk between Diosa and Stephen M____'s front porch. Tall and broad shouldered, he had thick, black hair, a strong jaw and a brooding, thick brow, large hands. He wore a dark, Italian-made suit and soft leather shoes; the styling was unmistakable. She'd never fallen in love at first sight, but now the thrill of him ripped through her; she felt him in her eyes, her lips, her breasts, her cunt. From his dark eyes she felt the overwhelming and surprising glue of wordless sympathy, not passion, but passionate sympathy. He took her in his arms.

They are on horseback down La Avinida de los Muertos in Teotihuacan. She remembers from a dream of her future. The sun is rising and Quetzalcoatl crawls up the steps of his temple. There, they

110

make love on the back of a sweating mare; they paint each other with her hot, white foam. He holds her on his lap like Shiva holds Sarasvati, his tongue in her mouth, his finger in her ass, his penis like Zeno's arrow, her orgasm like a parallel infinity. Later, when he holds her afloat on a lotus in a sea of milk and soma, his body smooth, supple, and tight as steel, he places the words of forever love in her heart, in his heart.

"Every moment I possess you I save a life," he tells her.

"Why not save the world?" she says to him.

"A life," he says. "Isn't that a world?

"An archangel tickles my shoulder with flame. In a few years you will ask for my phone number."

He laughs. He blinks. Years pass.

"I'll call you every night," he whispers, "when you are in your deepest sleep, I'll be there, behind the nothing, deeper than the dark."

"Ask what you like," Diosa says.

"What I like is
simply the notion
of parting at death
of seeing you in the darkness
of wearing an
afterlife dress
and escaping forgiveness."

Around them it is as quiet as a galaxy. She knows that this is not love. That you can't love immortality. She feels him, piece by infinite piece falling away in ecstatic joy.

"I am only a messenger," he says. "All of me is borrowed." His whispering shatters stars. "Do you believe in angels?"

"Ghosts," she says. "My love makes ghosts."

"Your true love is loving," he says, "loving a path of ghosts. Running toward you."

"You can't even save lives," she says.

"For a little while," he says, "you have saved mine from the tedium of immortality. But you, you will possess nothing you desire, yet you will soon fall in love forever. It will last but a blink." He put his beautiful hand on her breasts. "Your heart will ache with it."

She kisses him again. His lips are softer than music. She rises to him, and he vanishes.

Stephen M_____ stood at his door, his lank body gray behind a screen.

She didn't believe in the divine, unless it unrolled in a pile of words, refined, excavated like the fossils of souls. But neither did she believe in souls. For a moment she remembers the future, sees a man that she loves holding a small gray cat named Sartre; the cat dies, the lover dies, the world turns upside down with simple affection and it saves no one. Existence precedes essence and what are either but nothingness? Yet there, on the firing line between nothingness and the divine, where nothingness grumbles like thunder and the divine dissipates like mist, there, angels lurk, or ghosts, ephemeral and eternal, like math, and when they visit everything changes, and when everything changes, nothing changes; like satori the specialness of your life drops out from under your feet, the unrealized miracle of every moment disappearing flash by flash. One day, Diosa would have a daughter; she stands now, the visage of Stephen M_____ behind the gray screen, and remembers the future and she shudders, and at twenty-three the girl, her daughter, more beautiful than the Northern Lights, turns to her, points to a map of Australia and says, Mother, I'm moving to Mars, and twenty-three years of Diosa's life disappears like a dream, and the difference between dream and memory disappear like the difference between nothingness and angels; God's gifts fall away in ragged breaths; the heart aches, death lingers, like shadows, like joy, like dream, like memory. How could she know, standing there, that she stood atop a mountain of time? Because all life was momentous, it was hard to know the moment. She hesitated. How many years had she been standing there?

Stephen M____, America's greatest living poet, stared through the screen at the most beautiful woman in the world, knowing that in front of his face she'd made love to an angel, though it only elevated his passion. For what is an angel? A being of essence only (sayeth Aquinas) possessing neither body nor mind, living, like the Tibetan deities, airlessly, between humanity and infinity, arbitrary messengers of benevolence and violence; yet being essence only, they do not exist, nothingness exists more. Though Stephen M____ was touched by one once and his poetry, briefly, rose to the sublime. In front of his face, he felt the angel touching her. Now, when he gazed at Diosa, he fell into her eyes as had a thousand men in a thousand years, though he wasn't jealous of her body but her legacy, her poems yet unwritten that had already touched the adjoining divine and brought his passion to the tilt.

From that moment onward his life changed. He came down from Rune Mountain to a village celebrating destiny. He realized another life. His own. He married a girl, tended a garden, raised sons, one of whom became a poet and married Stephen M____'s grandmother. They tried to have children eight times but six died at childbirth (On the night that Roscoe watched the ghosts parade with Ellenberg in front of his house, Stephen M ____'s grandmother pushed a carriage of twins and led the others by the hand), of the two survivors the daughter became a palm reader in Prague, the son, Stephen M_____'s father, migrated to Newfoundland and became a fisherman. Stephen M_____ would never get on a boat, but sailed the cryptic ocean of mind. Now, Diosa in front of him, glowing, he knew his life stream was one among a million, if all his own, strewn with possibility; he knew his future could be something else, somewhere else. He could leave his life, his wife; he could let everything go and fall in love again.

"Diosa," whispered Stephen M_____, America's greatest living poet. "Love me, Diosa."

She approached the porch. She walked up the steps. She held a bouquet of white flowers like a bride. He opened the door and took her hand. She met his steel gray eyes.

"Stephen," she said. "I can't be your lover."

AND WATCH YOU DIE

IN BANFF, NAOMI CLIMBED a glacier and was buried in an avalanche. On Mackinaw Island, riding on the history of desperate suicides, she drove her motorcycle off the bridge. In Thunder Bay she got in a dice game with a bartender, and went home with him, left him in the morning for a boat captain from Sault St. Marie and was gored by a bull moose on Michipcoten Island. She caught up with Roscoe outside Trois Riviere, Quebec.

"You're a lousy date," Roscoe told her.

"It's keeping you interested," she said. She slept with him that night. She screamed so loudly the Mounties came to his tent. She grinned at them. "Can I get a photo with a Mountie?" she said. Anyway, she couldn't.

"At least they didn't shoot you," said Roscoe.

"Would you like them to?"

"To what?"

"The notion of parting at death," she said. "I give it to you in abundance."

He had a thought. Why not say it? "You're not Gabe," he said.

"Not even close."

"But you know him?"

She sat in his lap, faced him, wrapped him between her thighs, put her tongue on his, opened herself to him again. "If I told you your love could save me, would you love me?"

"How much would you need?"

She laughed, leaning back to push him against her G-spot.

They never made it to Quebec City. But in lower Manhattan she was taken down by gang war crossfire on B Street while trying to score dope. She found him in Philadelphia where she crawled up the statue of George Washington, folded up in his arms and French kissed him. She was shot by a livid patriot who was exonerated. In Pittsburgh she was mowed down by an old woman assuming a "Pittsburgh Left." In his way, he was beginning to love her, to see her coming and going as metaphor, to see their love making as a dance, of course, with death. But where could it go? Camping in a sunflower field in Kansas, a truck bore down on his tent. He tried to pull her out, but she refused. As he finally rolled away the vehicle slammed through the tent, then turned around and headed back as Roscoe retrieved Naomi's pistol and shot out the tires. When the truck lumped to a halt Roscoe walked to the driver's side and raised the pistol. The window came down. Their eyes met. The world came apart. It was him. Dead or alive he'd returned.

"Each death?" Roscoe said.

"Would you like to sell me your shadow, Roscoe?" he said. "Or your soul?"

In those eyes he saw the army officer who taught him to shoot. He remembered other lives, wars, deaths, whether he'd lived them or not. There was no way out. He had unwittingly submitted to this cycle and long since stopped believing in anything but Naomi's deaths, increasingly falling in love with their reunions, her returns. In that way he was no different than the devil in front of him, her other lover, now he knew.

He lowered the gun. The man got out of the truck, walked to Naomi's bike and drove away. When Roscoe went to the crumbled tent, as he expected, she was gone.

She met him at the National Monument outside Grand Junction, Colorado. He'd parked his bike and made a precipitous rock climb to the top of a narrow, orange spine that fell upward into space like a cathedral spire. She was there, waiting.

"Don't jump," he said.

"Not yet," said Naomi. She spread her arms. "I just got here!"

He thought of Gabe now. He thought of spontaneity and fire, trains and graveyards, fate and the denial of fate.

"You're going to Salt Lake City," she said.

"Inevitably," he said, because eventually everything is driven toward what happens, whatever that happens to be.

"It doesn't matter," Naomi said. "It could be Elmira or Gainesville or Bowling Green."

"Not Bowling Green," he said. "I've been to Bowling Green."

"You miss the point. You're going to fall in love, hard and deep.

Then your life will pass in a flash, and you'll come to the day when you'll wish you could die as often and easily as I do. But remember me then as your second-greatest love.

She came to him. He held her and she wept. "Love me," she said.

"And watch you die."

"The ghost forever in your wake."

Reasonlessly, he whispered, "Now and at the time of my death."

"Our death," she said. "Amen."

They kissed. "I love you," she said. "Don't leave me." And then, "You must leave me."

"I love you, too," Roscoe said to her. Then he turned and leapt from the cliff.

THEIR EYES

SHE NO LONGER WANTED to be the Queen of Poetry. She wanted to be a poet. She wanted to transform and be transformed by the written word, its miracles, its mysteries; write for the chorus of the immortals, join them in their moments of bliss called heaven. Could he not teach her that? Mentor her to the cusp of the spiritual? Be rid of the burden and their madness, their desire? Of sex? Of love? Enter together the infinite quest, the soul's passion, truth and beauty in separate graves?

In a word, no. Worse than being spurned was this, the reason she spurned him, leaving him for the lover who had left him long ago. That he had been weaned from passion and elided into craft and lust, fallen to admiration and fame, awards and wine and power. No one jumps ship, he told himself, without already choosing a place to land, another ship. No one flies. No one swims.

"I will destroy you," he told her before he even realized that he'd played his last card, like a teenager threatening suicide, the difference between fifteen and fifty, but equally pitiable and powerless.

How could those words, mere words, not change everything? Would she sleep with him now that he'd exposed his power? Now that he'd already set the terms of its beginning and end? How different was it from a Mormon patriarch taking his fourth teenage wife? A sultan filling his harem with concubines? I offer you my wings, the small of my back in mid-flight, as long as my love holds out. He saw it. He said, "I'm sorry."

She saw it, too, but chose the apology over the threat and stayed when she should have run, thinking that he meant the latter. How could anyone believe the other? When he in fact—when he saw her soften—knew that he'd gained forbearance, forced overtime, obtained a continuance in his seduction. She was there. She was his student now. There was time.

But not much time. Less than he thought. She didn't come to him for love and in a matter of weeks his feeling about her work began to change. He saw it as pointlessly disruptive, girlish, senseless in its self-conscious avoidance of profundity, something he once found profound, and he said so, he told everyone.

Kevorkian saw it. "Falling is not flight," she said, and fled. She packed up her kids and moved to Berkeley. Each night Diosa wept. Everyday, Stephen M____, America's greatest living poet, brought out his scythe. He would bring her to him, if he must, with cruelty. With no other choices, she would come to him. An old, old story. He ridiculed her in the poetry workshops, handed out fellowships and awards to her peers, sat as judge for poetry prizes, handing them down to his other apprentices. Soon, everyone figured it out. Faculty avoided her, students, too, but for a handful of drunken fiction writers. One night, drunk and depressed, she almost slept with one but stopped when he clutched his chest, shuddered and sagged. She called 911.

Enter the kindly, married, middle-aged playwright and gambler, Professor Martin "The Crane" Steel.

"Become a playwright," he said to her. "Let's have lunch and talk about it."

This was the new world where lunch was a yellow brick road.

"I'm leaving the program," she said over a chardonnay (that he brought to the restaurant and paid an enormous fee for corkage).

"Write a play," he said. "I'll read it. I'm sure it will be good."

And she did and it was. It was called *Wave's Home*, about a childless couple who run a home for pregnant teenagers. They place the babies for a fee on both ends and Wave always buys a Lincoln Continental with the profits. He keeps the cars in their backyard. His wife, Myrtle, keeps a handsome, imaginary, piano-playing lover who appears on stage and accompanies her poetic soliloquies in which she longs for a child of her own. For her part, when she's not quibbling with Wave, she's subverting him among the three, live-in pregnant teenagers who she convinces to keep their babies. Of course, that makes Wave pretty mad. Climax ahead. Crane fell in love with the play and got Diosa a residency at Sundance where TV actors like Chuck Norris and Didi Conn workshopped it. Crane placed Diosa in a cabin with a bedroom right next to his. Nothing new there. She kept him at a professional distance. He was more patient and less cruel than Stephen M_____.

The play ran and sold out each night for three months at the Salt

Lake Acting Company. It won play of the year. Now, rising from the dregs of the University Writing Program, she was a municipal celebrity. In the midst of this, a run of adoring actors, directors, producers, and dramaturges, male and female, but by now she was 27, wary and aloof. She couldn't be aware, how could she, that her affection was fate, that her love, however brief, or tentative, or desperate, opened the gates of hell. Who could ever surmise that from the goodness of her heart sprang death? Wasn't that God's domain, to create out of joy and love and then to watch those creations suffer, wither, die?

But more, it became increasingly apparent that she didn't have to love them at all, not even like them, not even touch them. In the world of dramatic arts, over the weeks of rehearsals, intimacy exploded everywhere; lovers on stage became lovers in life, as did rivals and enemies become rivals and enemies; the director loved your play, conquered your play, fell in love with you, fell out of love, though unlike poets they didn't lose their souls. Her leading man at Sundance, a crime show star from Toronto, merely stole a kiss, but drowned in an ice fishing accident in north Ontario. In thirty seconds or thirty years the moment came whether she loved them or not. Martin "The Crane" Steel, who pursued Diosa with feverish, unrequited subtlety, got caught counting cards at the Flamingo Casino in Las Vegas. When Ron Cotto faced him at the Black Jack table, the vision of Diosa, a Venus in white silk, danced between them. Like samurai connected by karmic wrath they were both found shot to death, Cotto near the trash containers behind the Flamingo on the Strip, Crane in the alley behind the Golden Nugget, downtown. Though miles apart, each was felled by a bullet from the other's gun.

Diosa grew tired of the flitting love, the quick heat, but more and worse, that each director, dramaturge, and even actor, twisted and turned, interpreted and rewrote her words. In the end, each time, the play was no longer hers. She longed for the subtle ecstasy of lyric.

> *There is generosity in darkness* (she wrote)
> *unmatched by the garden's mallows*
> *and plums. You have to*
>
> *go to hell*
>
> *to be healed by it —*
> *while the earth above you blisters and*
> *listens. You must   go there*
> *for love*
> *You must go there for* sound that dwells
> in the space within the heart

She longed for poetry.

Then one of the other greatest living poets in America, one of the next generation, ten years younger than Stephen M_____, the intoxicating and intoxicated poet, Harry Heaven, came to Salt Lake City and the University of Utah. Here's the thing. She loved his poetry before she met him. He was from Fresno, a dreamland away in California, a hand picked heir of Phil Levine, along with superstar William St. James. She met him at a party. She wore all white, from her fur hat to her high heels, her white skirt mid-thigh. His brow slouched, his lips sneered, his glasses fell over his nose, a bevy of female poets at his elbows, his half-open eyes, brown as daylight, deep as song, slurched over her.

"I know your work," he said to her. "Valbuena loved you."

It's a small galaxy.

"My son from my first marriage is visiting," he said to her. "I could use some help."

The young poets at his elbows swooned. Maybe they should take up playwriting.

She didn't plan to love him or even like him. He had no plans at all. They had lunch. She put his kid on a swing. The kid left town. Heaven put a line of cocaine on her inner thigh and snorted it up to her mons, then licked her. He wasn't even good at it. Kind of abstract and it made her numb.

"Come back to the poetry program," he said, his voice impossibly languid. "I love you."

But what was the love of a poet? What was the love of anyone?

Having learned a few tricks from Gabe, Roscoe floated down to his motorcycle and drove to Salt Lake City. When he got there he looked for a party; that's how you did it. Stephen M____ was out of town and his daughter was throwing herself a big party for turning twenty-one. In attendance, her new friend Dorna, the niece of the recently deposed Shah of Iran. Her family had fled to Paris and now, interestingly, Salt Lake City. How did that happen? Regardless, she was Persian and spoke French. French women loved Roscoe. In the future they would follow him around Paris, moon over him in cafes, stalk him in museums. Dorna had long, thick black hair, dark brown eyes. Roscoe entered the huge house, found a beer. He wandered upstairs to take a leak. Dorna met him at the top of the stairs when he left the bathroom.

"You will be my first real American cowboy," she said.

"I'm not a cowboy," Roscoe said.

"My first real one," Dorna said.

She took his hand. Found a bedroom. That was that. She was young; a bit over-zealous. Her family lived on Capital Hill in what could best be described as a compound—there were a lot of them in Salt Lake City, most of them occupied by polygamists—which explained the why Salt Lake City thing—high stone walls surrounded by tall, thick shrubs, inside the walls, lots of trees, a cavernous house of twisting hallways and studio apartments, everywhere, women, some draped in brown cloth, head to toe, others not.

"My aunts," Dorna said.

"That's a lot of aunts," Roscoe said.

Dorna had her own studio apartment inside there. So did each aunt. Hers had a door that opened to a swimming pool. While Roscoe sunned himself by the pool, the brown-draped women brought him fruit, nuts, olives, cheese, pitas and wine. They asked him what he needed.

"Who's calling the shots around here?" Roscoe asked Dorna.

She ran her finger from his collarbone to his waist, then put her hand on his genitals. He got hard. "Besides me?" she said.

"Some man?" Roscoe said.

"My mother is here," Dorna said. "Would you like a hamburger?"

"Your father?" Roscoe said.

"France," she said. "Switzerland." She put her hand on his chest. "Do you like me?"

"I don't know you."

"But you fuck me."

"You fuck me," Roscoe said. Roscoe didn't know it, but he was on the verge of something. In fact, he'd been on the verge of something for quite a long time. If he stepped outside he could see Salt Lake City buzzing below him, the Eagle Gate, the Mormon Temple, Moroni golden and blowing atop its spear. Was he thirty years old? He might be. Maybe he should start keeping track of things. Dorna left to fetch more wine. He lay in the sun. Where could this go? Why had he never asked himself that before? If he blinked now thirty years would pass; no miracle, it happens to everyone; he felt gray wings bristling on his back, the lawn hissing, his self expanding. Samsara was Nirvana. His insides bigger than his outsides, he was ready to take flight.

Dorna eating a hot dog, returned with his chardonnay. "Want a hot dog?" she said.

He took a bite of hers. The Heinz ketchup made him think of Pittsburgh, trash collecting, graveyards, trains.

"Come with me to Paris," Dorna said. "I'll give you whatever you want. Money, money, money. You'll be free." She sat on him, her long hair falling down. "Let's fuck," she said. And they did. But he was already dreaming of someone else.

Harry Heaven placed a line of cocaine in her cleavage. Snorted it. Licked her nipples. His tongue made them numb. He couldn't really get very hard, but he sure could party. One day, after he was dead—an overdose of heroin, booze, and coke, his heart bursting—all the once-girl poets, and plenty older ones too, would pull out their Harry Heaven merit badges, their love affairs with him entwined in their elegies, but only Diosa would leave a scar on his soul. He bunched her breasts in his palm. She disliked herself for it, but she loved that feeling, her breasts encupped. Worse, she still loved his poetry. When she was away from him, she heard him singing in sonorous depth, of loss and pain, images falling upon her like ashes, his innocence falling upon her like ashes.

"Marry me," he said.

The most absurd propositions sometimes made the most sense. His son from his first marriage was nine. His second marriage had just broken up; that woman was in the program, now a student of Stephen M____'s. She knew, as well, that he had a girlfriend, a tall brunette who supposedly helped him break his coke habit. But poets live inside love and myth. And now she had re-entered; once the mistress of Stephen M____, whether true or not. Then the Aphrodite of Sundance. The wife of Harry Heaven? Inside that she felt herself disappearing. Maybe she needed to disappear.

She rolled onto Harry Heaven. Let her breasts drop, her hair. She rubbed on his pelvis. Stared into his eternal brown eyes.

"I love you," he said to her. "Black stars, sullen evening, shadows."

"I love you, too," she whispered, as if, even then, falling into a heartbreaking infidelity.

That afternoon they got up and strolled through the aviary in Liberty Park. He took her hand. Why not marry Harry Heaven. What better way to re-enter the poetry world. What better way to confront Stephen M____. She turned and kissed Heaven. "Tomorrow," she said. "We'll get married tomorrow."

Roscoe left the Persian compound the next morning. He drove his bike out to the salt flats, the air screaming. He stopped at the lake, the air full of moist salt, the mist over the water rising like a ghost over the desert, the brown Oquirrh Mountains rolling west to Nevada. He didn't know why he turned back for Salt Lake City, possibly because it was the most absurd choice, perhaps because it appeared futureless. He drove north to Orem and from a bridge watched the rumbling of freight trains. He stood in front of each locomotive, letting them pass through him, then mounted his bike again and drove to the big graveyard near the center of Salt Lake City, walked through the alleys of obelisks, Young, Smith, Cannon, each surrounded by multiple stones that said only "Mother," each mother surrounded by dozens of tiny graves. He didn't find an Ellenberg, but in the search itself he found himself in that moment again, a little boy seeing a ghost, between the two of them, a dazzling blue-eyed girl, no, goddess. That was enough. He drove downtown to the train station with its mural of the Union and Pacific locomotives meeting in Utah to complete the transcontinental railroad. The station sat behind the Temple. He bought a train ticket to New York City. He'd wile away the days at a window, watching the country go by, dreaming.

He had a few hours to wait, so he found a shop to store his bike. Maybe he'd come back for it. Maybe not. Then he wandered to nearby Liberty Park. He strolled through the aviary. Thought of Plato's aviary analogy in the *Theaetetus*. Good old philosophy. How could you go into an aviary of numbered birds looking for the answer to six plus six, looking for the twelve bird and walk out with bird thirteen? He was looking at the ravens, the black birds. Looking for bird thirteen.

He spotted a man and a young woman. They walked hand in hand, moving languidly near a fountain. They kissed. Their hands left each other's, finger tips to finger tips, like dancers, and they parted. "Tomorrow," the girl said. "We'll marry tomorrow." He watched as she walked away. The man's chest heaved. The girl wore a short dress, brown and black horizontal stripes. It would stay in his mind until he died.

Diosa left Harry Heaven there in Liberty Park, her mind filled with endless impossibilities. She looked in her bag for her car keys. She looked up. Saw Roscoe only a few feet away. And around them, an explosion, a cacophony of bird sound, as if she'd carried it inside her since the first morning behind Ruth sparrow's cottage. Near them, behind a fence, a gigantic emu squawked and twisted his head, his eye reflecting Roscoe, then Diosa, as if he were trying to gather them both, somehow, in that retina. He pecked at Roscoe who gently put a fist on the tip of his beak. The bird opened his mouth. Roscoe slapped him and the bird recoiled.

"So that's how you do it," Diosa said.

Roscoe watched the sky above Salt Lake City turn to fire, though it was really Diosa's hair subduing thought and phenomena in great gasps, her blue eyes changing the cosmos moment by moment.

"I know you," he said.

"Have you been looking for me?"

"All my life."

She spun from him until she stopped in front of the cage of a huge Peruvian Condor. The bird spread his wings. They stretched to the breadth of the cage, at least twelve feet. Diosa reached for the rusted cage door lock, took it in her hand and snapped it open.

"Strength of an angel," she whispered as the bird dropped from his perch and strode out, taking in the whole of his sad imprisonment.

"Do you think he can fly?" said Diosa.

"I can," Roscoe said.

"Me too," Diosa said. "Anyone can."

The great black bird knelt in front of them. He spread his wings, once, twice, then took to the air. Soon high above them, they followed him with their eyes as he swooped over the Eagle Gate, over Capital

Hill, and then to the Temple where he circled Moroni's spire, the golden angel perched atop and on the verge of unleashing the blast that would awaken all the dead. The bird let out a painful wail and then returned, landing in front of them. All that had ever happened and all that would ever happen sprung from under the condor's wings. Everything came to this. Everything left from this. It was impossible, bathed in all this inevitability, that anyone could know what would happen next.

"I'm marrying Harry Heaven tomorrow," Diosa said. But she spun again, into Roscoe's arms, then away, and then back into his arms again. "Tomorrow," she whispered.

Yet he kissed her. And for the first time, as their lips parted from the kiss, their eyes truly met.

Roscoe whispered in return. "All great loves must turn their backs on heaven."

The condor spread his wings.

ABOUT THE AUTHOR

Chuck Rosenthal is the author of nine previous novels, a memoir, two books of Magic Journalism, and the co-author of two books of poetry. He lives in Topanga Canyon with the poet Gail Wronsky.

www.ingramcontent.com/pod-product-compliance
Lightning Source LLC
Chambersburg PA
CBHW021022120726
47905CB00009B/3143